A Most Discreet Inquiry
(The Regent Mysteries, Book 2)

The Regent Mysteries continue with Captain Jack and Lady Daphne. *With His Lady's Assistance* (Book 1 of The Regent Mysteries) was named a finalist in the 2012 International Digital Awards contest for long historical.

D1614162

An Improper Proposal

"Wonderfully Crafted... Highly recommended... 5 stars"
– *Huntress Reviews*

"Bolen does a wonderful job building simmering sexual tension between her opinionated, outspoken heroine and deliciously tortured, conflicted hero." – *Booklist of the American Library Association*

One Golden Ring

"*One Golden Ring*...has got to be the most PERFECT Regency Romance I've read this year." – *Huntress Reviews*

"Totally delightful, beautifully sensual, and endearingly romantic love story."
– *Romance Designs*

The Counterfeit Countess

"This story is full of romance and suspense. . . No one can resist a novel written by Cheryl Bolen. Her writing talents charm all readers. Highly recommended reading! 5 stars!"
– *Huntress Reviews*

"This is a delightful Regency romp complete with matchmaking, traitor hunting and finding just the right man when you least expect it. Bolen pens a sparkling tale and readers will adore her feisty heroine, the arrogant, honorable Warwick and a wonderful cast of supporting characters."
– *RT BookCLUB*

A Lady By Chance

"Cheryl Bolen has done it again with another sparkling Regency romance" – *In Print*

The Four-Leaf Clover

"Cheryl Bolen's Four-Leaf Clover is too adorable for words."
– *Mrs. Giggles reviews*

Cheryl Bolen's Books

Regency Historical Romance:

The Brides of Bath Series
The Bride Wore Blue
With His Ring
The Bride's Secret
To Take This Lord
Love In The Library
A Christmas in Bath

House of Haverstock Series
Lady by Chance
Duchess by Mistake
Countess by Coincidence
Ex-Spinster by Christmas

Brazen Brides Series
Counterfeit Countess
His Golden Ring
Oh What A (Wedding) Night
Miss Hastings' Excellent London Adventure
A Birmingham Family Christmas

The Regent Mysteries Series
With His Lady's Assistance
A Most Discreet Inquiry
The Theft Before Christmas
An Egyptian Affair

The Earl's Bargain
My Lord Wicked
His Lordship's Vow
Christmas Brides (Three Regency Novellas)
Marriage of Inconvenience
A Duke Deceived

Romantic Suspense:
Falling For Frederick

Texas Heroines in Peril Series
   Protecting Britannia
   Murder at Veranda House
   A Cry In The Night
   Capitol Offense

World War II Romance:
It Had to Be You

American Historical Romance:
A Summer To Remember (3 American Romances)

A MOST DISCREET INQUIRY

(The Regent Mysteries, Book 2)

Cheryl Bolen

$\mathcal{C}$hapter 1

Not since the next-to-eldest of Lord Sidworth's daughters snared the Duke of Lankersham had Sidworth House been in such a dither. Footmen in scarlet livery, madly scurrying chambermaids, and a contingent of supervisory-sounding servants were practically tripping over themselves readying the earl's home for the day's momentous occasion: the wedding of Daughter Number One.

With no intention of criticism toward the lady in question, none of those anticipating the happy event had ever thought to see the day Lady Daphne Chalmers would wed.

This lack of expectations had not been precipitated because the lady did not have pedigree, nor because she could not bring a respectable dowry, nor because she was not amiable. She possessed all these qualities in abundance. Those who vastly admired Lady Daphne (and there were many of those, to be sure) could not deny that the poor girl—no, girl was not precisely the right descriptor—the poor woman, was a hopeless spinster. She had been on the shelf so long that a new generation of debutants had made Lady Daphne's group as distant a memory as her father's powdered wig.

Yet today Lady Daphne was getting married.

It had been expected Lord Sidworth would be so desperate to marry off the eldest of his six daughters that he would lower his aim. Initially, he had thought only the finest aristocrat in all the three kingdoms worthy of his firstborn—and favorite.

Now, though, Lord Sidworth had given his consent for his beloved Daphne to wed a man with far fewer recommendations than the earl would once have considered *barely acceptable*. Lady Daphne's intended was *not* an aristocrat. Nor was he possessed of fortune. Nor did he hold a commanding rank in the Prince of Wales' Royal Light Hussars. He was a mere captain.

Captain Jack Dryden even had the effrontery—while begging His Royal Highness's pardon—to turn down a more exalted title urged upon him by both Lord Sidworth and by the Prince Regent himself. The stubborn captain would accept neither an aristocratic title nor a higher rank in his majesty's service, both offered by the Regent, who admired Captain Dryden excessively.

The captain further aggravated his future father-in-law by refusing the enormous dowry Lord Sidworth wished to settle upon Lady Daphne. (Captain Dryden did finally capitulate enough to accept a dowry that would allow his wife-to-be to live in a style not abhorrent to one raised as an earl's daughter.)

Despite the great disparity in stations of the intended couple, everyone in the *ton* thought Lady Daphne had done very well for herself. Both the Prince Regent and the Duke of Wellington credited Captain Dryden with all manner of heroic activities, including saving the Regent's life. Men envied the captain's tall, well-formed body while admiring his skill with the sword.

And women. . . well, women had a propensity to flutter eyelashes, drop hankies, and positively swoon when in the presence of the exceedingly handsome man whom Daphne herself had dubbed Captain Sublime.

Those not well acquainted with the happy couple no doubt thought Captain Jack Dryden a great fortune hunter. Or they might think him a hanger-on to aristocratic coattails. Neither could be further from the truth.

Those who knew Daphne and Jack knew theirs was a true love match.

Quite recently, while investigating threats against the Prince Regent, Daphne and Jack—who had not been previously acquainted—had been forced to pose as lovers, and their ruse ended up being anything but.

Initially, Jack had not been attracted to Lady Daphne. He lamented that he was going to have to feign attraction to a bespectacled woman who was tall, skinny, and in possession of the most unruly head of hair imaginable. Therefore, the incendiary effect that particular lady's presence began to wreak upon his passions had been as shocking to him as would have been the sprouting of a third leg.

Equally as shocking was the discovery that the noble lady was in no way adverse to uniting herself with a captain of such unfortunate origins. The lady was actually adamant that Jack was the most noble man she had ever known. He knew he was neither noble nor worthy of a woman as wonderful as Daphne, but what was he to do when the Regent himself declared they belonged together?

On this most blissful of wedding days, Cornelia—Daphne's duchess sister—accompanied by her much-taller twin, swept through the door of Sidworth House, smiling broadly. "I declare, Virginia," she said to her sister, "I cannot wait to see Daphne in the wedding dress I had made for her." The two did not pause long enough to even take off their velvet bonnets but began to race upstairs toward Lady Daphne's bedchamber.

"Even Daphne would have to look lovely in *that* dress," Virginia said, "for I do believe I've never seen anything lovelier."

Cornelia nodded. "I will own, it was difficult not to claim something so vastly beautiful for myself, but I did so want Daphne to look . . .well, to look as lovely as possible on her wedding day." She frowned. "Especially since she'll be standing next to that ---"

Virginia paused on the step and stared into her sister's brown eyes—the only feature the twins had in common. "That paragon of masculinity?"

Cornelia, Duchess of Lankersham, nodded, still frowning. (Lamentably, her own duke was not only *not* a paragon of masculinity but was a bit on the portly side and in sad need of hair on top his shiny head.)

In front of Lady Daphne's door, the twins paused. "I just know Daphne will be radiantly beautiful today," Virginia said.

Her face lifted into a smile, the duchess nodded in agreement and swept open the door to Daphne's bedchamber.

And she gasped. (This was *not* a gasp of acute admiration.)

Virginia shrieked.

Still in her night shift, spectacles slipping down her nose, Daphne straddled a wooden chair that had been strategically placed in front of a window. There, with a paint brush in her right hand and copious amounts of brown paint splotching her face, she sat before an easel displaying a still-wet painting of a horse.

She looked up at her sisters and smiled.

Cornelia's lips compressed, and her eyes narrowed. "Pray, why are you not dressed?"

Concurrently, Virginia asked, "Whatever are you doing, Daphne?"

"In the middle of the night I got the brilliant idea of painting a portrait of dear Jack's charger as a wedding gift to him." She leaned back and surveyed the portrait of the roan gelding sporting a blue and silver shabracque. "I do believe it's one of my best efforts. And you know how Jack loves that beast!"

"I could almost understand it," Virginia mumbled to the duchess, "were she giving her bridegroom her own miniature, but a horse?"

The duchess was too angry to form a response. She stood in the center of Daphne's bedchamber and began to scream. "Mama! Papa!"

From her frantic tone, her parents (and all the servants, as well) would surely believe the room was being consumed by flames.

In seconds, Lord and Lady Sidworth burst into the chamber.

"Oh, dear," Lady Sidworth said, shaking her head when she realized the bride had neglected to don her bridal dress. "I should have insisted my maid come to her this morning, but Daphne was so opposed to the idea!"

Daphne glared, first at the duchess, then at her mother. "Must you speak of me in the third person? I *am* right here. And you, Mama, know I don't care a fig about beauty and having a lady's maid. The wife of an army captain cannot afford so unnecessary an expenditure."

"You must own, Mama," the duchess said, "there would be nary a thing for a maid of Daphne's to do. Look at her! She hasn't even brushed her hair—not that she ever does." Cornelia stomped up to her elder sister. "I daresay a brush hasn't touched your hair since last night."

Daphne gazed into Cornelia's angry face. "Of course not, silly. Why would I dress my hair before I finished with the painting? You know what a mess I make when I paint."

Cornelia sighed. "For god's sake, Daphne! It's your wedding day."

An almost ethereal smile came over Lady Daphne's face. She quite possibly would have looked pretty, were it not for the brown paint marring her creamy complexion. "I assure you I haven't forgotten that."

"But, Pet," Lord Sidworth said in a gentle voice as he approached his most beloved daughter, "you were supposed to leave for the church in five minutes."

"We'll just have to keep Captain Dryden waiting!" Cornelia said. "We must see that Daphne's made presentable."

The bride-to-be's mouth gaped open. "I did not realize I was to leave in five minutes. However will I get all this paint off?"

Though no one had noticed her leaving, the other twin returned to the chamber with a moist cloth. "I'll just dab this spirit of turpentine on your face and hands, dear love, and get rid of that brown paint as quick as you please."

"Daphne cannot show up at her wedding smelling of that horrible turpentine!" Cornelia protested.

"If we follow it with soap and water and liberally apply my rose water afterward, I think it will work," Lady Sidworth said. "It wouldn't at all do for Daphne to stink up the church."

"I wonder if Jack likes the smell of rose water," Daphne commented as Virginia gently removed the paint from her nose. "He's become most fond of my spear mint scent."

Cornelia rolled her eyes. "I fail to see why you won't wear perfume like other women. You're so exasperating!"

"I am not like other women," Daphne answered with a shrug. "I have no interest whatsoever in what is fashionable."

"And Captain Dryden loves her just as she is," Lord Sidworth said with a pride like the barnyard rooster who'd just sired a peacock. He strolled to the chamber door. "I shall leave you ladies, but please hurry. I'll send word to the church that you'll be slightly late."

"I don't care what my elder sister wants," Cornelia said with a great deal of authority. "Pru's to come here straight away and help pin up that unruly mass of hair on Daphne's head. I won't have her looking like that on her wedding day."

Lady Sidworth went to the bell pull. "I'll ring for her right now."

"I declare, Cornelia," Daphne said, glaring at her sister, "you treat all of us—including your very own mother—as if you're some deity, and we're your subjects."

Virginia paused and examined Daphne to see if she had missed any spots. "She's right, *Your Grace.*"

Cornelia stomped her slippered foot. "If my good opinion is not needed, I'll just take myself off to St. George's!" She stormed from the bedchamber.

* * *

Standing with his brother at the front of St. George's, Jack kept searching the church's doorway. It really wasn't like Daphne to be late. Normally, she was one of those persons who has every single minute accounted for. Beforehand. Her sisters he could see being late because—being more interested in fashion and such than Daphne—they could get delayed trying on gowns and arranging hair or any number of things ladies of fashion did.

Yet the most fashionable of the six sisters, Cornelia, Duchess of Lankersham, was already there at the church. She and Lankersham had entered St. George's with the air of royal personages. After only the briefest nod in Jack's direction at the front of the church, they had strolled along the nave like a king and queen at coronation. No pew would do for them except the first. Jack found himself wondering if they chose it because it was the closest to the altar or if they did so because the duchess craved admiration.

There was much to admire, not only in her dark, petite beauty but also in her impeccable eye for all that was fashionable. Not that Jack considered himself particularly knowledgeable on matters of taste in women's clothing.

It was difficult for him to believe this haughty aristocrat and Daphne could have come from the same womb. While Daphne was tall, the duchess was short. While Daphne had no interest in fashion, the duchess lived for it. And while Daphne was no great beauty, the duchess was.

Cornelia entered the pew first. Her bald-headed duke came next. How uncharitable of Jack to think him bald. Lankersham was not completely bald. A circle of dark hair ringed his head, reminding Jack of a picture he'd seen of some friar—or was it a papist saint?

Jack's gaze came back to the front of the church and to the vicar in silken vestments who stood beside him. He favored the clergyman with a smile as he shrugged. His bride must be a half hour late now.

Daphne had insisted only family members be invited to the small wedding. Owing to his father's ill health, Jack's family was represented only by the one brother who stood beside him.

The Earl of Sidworth's family was much larger, and because of their class, all the aunts and uncles and cousins possessed London town houses for The Season, and since this happened to be The Season, there were enough members of Daphne's extended family to fill a fourth of the church.

As time stretched on, the guests' voices, respectfully quiet at first, began to fill the church with the drone of their chatter. Jack, too, contributed to the swell of voices when he turned to David and spoke. "I'm becoming worried about Daphne. She's never late."

"You know what women are when dressing their hair and that sort of thing."

Jack frowned. "It's obvious you haven't met Daphne."

Cheryl Bolen

His bride was a full three quarters of an hour late, but the wait was worth every minute. Joy pulsed into every crevice of his body when he looked up and saw Daphne sweep through the church doors on her father's arm. Her golden hair *was* dressed. And most becomingly. Normally a bushy mane, her hair was swept back from her slender face in the style of a Grecian goddess.

Next to her father, who was nearly as tall as Jack's six feet, two inches, Daphne didn't look so very tall. There was even a certain elegance about her today in the soft ivory gown that trailed behind her. As she drew closer, her sparkling green eyes met his and held. There was not another face in the kingdom he would rather behold, not another woman who stirred his lust like this boy-chested woman who about to become his wife.

She came to stand beside him, and he took her white-gloved hand. This was the happiest day of his life.

* * *

Throughout the nervous walk down the nave at St. George's, she looked at the dark-haired man she was about to marry. She thought she had never seen a more magnificent sight. He wore his regimentals, presenting a spotless appearance with his well-polished boots, crisp white breeches, and sparkling brass buttons against his red coat.

So many fleeting thoughts collided as she gazed upon him. How his tailor must marvel at cutting the cloth for such a man! Jack had been favored with wide shoulders, long trunk, and narrow waist. How could one as handsome as he have fallen in love with a bespectacled spinster such as she?

Their eyes met. Her heart stampeded as she peered into his flashing black eyes. Coming to stand beside him, she placed her hand in his and discovered hers was shaking.

Later, as Daphne recited her marriage vows, she realized she had never been happier. She could have looked the earth over and never found a man more to her liking. It was not just the perfection of his handsome appearance she had fallen in love with.

She loved his soul. He was the finest, most noble man in the three kingdoms. He was possessed of a quick intelligence and was well read. He was courageous. And he was modest.

Most of all, he loved her. Long before she allowed herself to acknowledge her love for him, she had known that he had fallen in love with her even when he thought an alliance between two from such dissimilar backgrounds impossible.

The very idea of being cherished by this wonderful man made her glow from the inside as they stood there, surrounded by those she loved most. Her hands linked with Jack's as they vowed to love one another until separated by death.

When he produced a simple gold band and slipped it on her finger, she was nearly overcome with the significance of this ceremony, this sacrament. Now she truly belonged to him. Her beloved Jack.

* * *

The Earl of Sidworth had offered them his own coach to transport the bride and groom from the church to the wedding breakfast at Sidworth House. Jack thought it was very good of Daphne's father to arrange for them to have these few minutes alone in the carriage before being accosted with a house full of Chalmers and Percy relations.

He and Daphne waved graciously from the coach window to those standing on the Hanover Square pavement surrounding St. George's. Until they were out of view. Then Jack lowered the velvet curtains, drew his wife into his arms, and began to kiss her rather passionately.

Though she had no vast experience in the art of kissing, Daphne was proving to be an apt pupil. He greatly looked forward to advancing her education in other amorous matters.

While his bride was emitting throaty little noises of appreciation, a great pounding of hooves and shouting bore down on their coach. Wheels skidded to a stop amid shrill whinnying from their horses. What the devil?

Their kiss hastily terminated, he flicked up the curtain to see what had brought their carriage to so sudden a stop. Their coach was surrounded by heavily armed hussars. The Regent's own regiment.

His first thought was that the French had attacked England on her own shores. Every man would be needed. As much as he did not want to leave his bride, he knew his duty was to England.

He threw open the coach door and disembarked. Quickly discerning which of the dozen men surrounding them was the highest ranking, he addressed that man. "Pray, Captain, explain why you stopped our coach on my wedding day."

"I am to give you this communiqué and escort you to an undisclosed location." He handed Jack a sealed letter.

It bore the Regent's seal.

Jack broke the seal and scanned the short letter written in what he believed to be the Regent's own hand on the sovereign's crested stationary.

My Dear Captain,

You are needed at once. My soldiers will escort you to your destination. It may be some days before you return to your bride. Tell no one, except Lady Daphne. I am sure your resourceful bride will think of some excuse to explain your absence.

It was signed by the Regent.

"We've taken the liberty of procuring your horse," the captain told Jack.

$\mathcal{C}$hapter 2

To Daphne's astonishment, they were fifteen minutes into the wedding breakfast before someone commented on the groom's absence. (The one person who would have known her to be lying—his brother—was obligated to return to Sussex immediately after the wedding ceremony.)

"Dearest," Lady Sidworth finally said, "Where is your husband?"

Daphne set down her fork, drew a deep breath, and lowered her brows to embellish her performance. "My poor Jack was determined to make it through the ceremony, but then the illness he's been fighting claimed him."

"How dreadful!" Lady Sidworth said as a chorus of other attendees agreed. "Whatever is the matter with him? He looked perfectly well."

Oh, yes! He most certainly did. "He woke up with mumps. You know what Jack is. He wouldn't dream of exposing all these people, and once he found out that I never had them, he insisted on quarantining himself. He wouldn't even allow himself to kiss me."

Her very breath thinned at the memory of their passionate kiss in the carriage. Pride swelled within her as she pictured Jack riding off on his mount to serve his country. She issued a forlorn sigh.

"Then your wedding trip to Addersley Priory won't take place, either?"

Daphne could have wept. "It doesn't look like it." She had so looked forward to rambling with Jack around the Sidworth ancestral country home in the Essex countryside. They were to have had the house all to themselves. They had planned long rides and lazy picnics and romantic evenings beside the fire.

Lady Sidworth spun around to face her husband. "Did you hear that, Sidworth? Captain Dryden has been quarantined with the mumps."

"Decent of him. I shouldn't like our Daf to get them. Still remember when Penworth came down with them at Eton. The fellow got a fat neck, ran fever, then the next thing we knew, they were carrying his dead body out the door. Frightfully upsetting to a nine-year-old lad."

"Now, Sidworth, you shouldn't say those things in front of Daphne. She'll worry herself sick over that dear husband of hers."

"Didn't one of our girls have the mumps?" inquired his lordship as he slathered marmalade onto his toast.

Lady Sidworth nodded. "The two youngest. Rosemary and Di. Remember, we sent the other girls off to your mother's so they wouldn't get them?"

He nodded. "Every one of us had them when we were growing up. Mother said I was by far the sickest. I don't remember it myself."

"That's because you don't remember anything unless it involves carrying off dead bodies." Lady Sidworth rolled her eyes and turned to face Daphne. "I suppose Captain Dryden's gone to your house."

Uh oh. Her mother would think he had gone to their new home, which wasn't new at all. The modest Chelsea house had been in the female branch of the Percy family for generations. Mama had passed it to Daphne upon her marriage, having decided another of her properties would be her dower house, should she ever become widowed. "Not actually," Daphne responded, trying to come up with a plausible explanation of Jack's whereabouts.

"What a pity. I was so hoping he was so we could have you here at Sidworth House for a few more nights." Lady Sidworth's gentle gaze fixed on her daughter. "It's very sad to relinquish one's firstborn."

Whew! Her parents hadn't even inquired about Jack's location! "Then I will be happy to continue on here at Sidworth House until Jack re---" She had started to say *returns*, but changed it to, "recuperates." She stabbed at her herring. "I shouldn't like to go to our home without Jack. Especially on our wedding night."

She was quickly losing her appetite. And her good humor. Why did she have to marry the most important man in British government? Had she married a lesser man, they would be on their way to Addersley Priory this very afternoon.

"I daresay it would be lonely at your new home all by yourself," Rosemary said. "I know I would be frightened if I were alone in that house at night. You haven't even procured servants yet, have you?"

A distracted look on her face, Daphne answered. "I have the one chambermaid."

Lady Sidworth directed her attention on her eldest daughter again. "Really, dearest, you must interview prospective servants."

"You know I don't like to do something at which I'm inept."

"Should you like me to assist?" Lady Sidworth asked.

"I should love it, my dearest mother!"

Daphne felt Cornelia's eyes on her. The duchess was at the opposite end of the long table and obviously felt deprived of the information regarding Jack's disappearance. A moment later, she left her half-eaten plate and quickly made it to the head of the table. "Wherever is the captain?"

Lady Sidworth answered. "He's come down with the mumps."

"Had to be quarantined," Lord Sidworth added.

Cornelia thrust hands to hips. "Where, pray tell?"

Daphne wished she could stuff her hard-cooked egg down her inquisitive sister's throat. "I daresay he's at his lodgings."

After the guests left, and after her married sisters returned to their homes with their husbands, and after she climbed into the same solitary bed she'd slept in every night for more than twenty years, Daphne grew melancholy.

This was her wedding night.

And she had no idea where her husband was or when she would see him again.

* * *

He was trying to be a professional about this. After all, Captain Jack Dryden was a professional soldier. Had been since he was seventeen years of age. Duty always came first. England always came first.

But that was before Daphne. He fleetingly wondered if he were given the choice of saving the lives of his comrades in arms or the life of one very slender, bespectacled young woman with remarkably unruly hair, which he would save.

He loved Daphne that much.

Which is what made this blasted assignment—if one could call it such—so deuced difficult. He felt wretched he'd had to leave her on their wedding day. As bad as that was, his hunger to see to her, to take her in his arms, was even worse. Four days it had been since they had married.

The first day was a bloody blur of being forced to depart London for Brighton—without being able to tell Daphne where he was going—and riding hell bent to leather to meet the Prince Regent at the Royal Marine Pavilion in that watering city. Jack's missive from the Prince Regent had hinted that Jack was needed, but alas, once Jack arrived at the sumptuous pavilion where the Prince spent much time, he was informed the Prince's arrival had been delayed.

Three of the most boring, frustrating days in his existence followed. The Prince still had not arrived. It was almost too painful to contemplate that by now he could have made love to his wife. The very thought of lying with her in their marriage bed accelerated his erratic breathing. He had best turn his thoughts to other, less exciting diversions.

The only diversion permissible was at the magnificent domed building known as the Royal Stables. The massive proportions of the two-storied giant rotunda rendered the Regent's own little palace across a smallish square of verdant lawn from it. . . well, little! Ringing the ground floor of the Royal Stables were rooms for sixty horses. Rooms, not stalls. Above them, ostlers and grooms resided.

In the center of the elegant and airy glass-domed building was an octagonal pool where the horses could drink. His Warrior would never want to leave! Jack was permitted to exercise Warrior each day in the adjoining Riding House.

But there, as at the Regent's Marine Pavilion where Jack had been assigned a guest room finer than any chamber in which he had ever spent a night, Jack felt a fish out of water. Whether at the Riding House or at the dinner table at the pavilion, Jack was the only guest not of the nobility. And he did not even have Daphne to show him which fork to use!

He was profoundly grateful on the morning of the fifth day when he was summoned to meet with the Prince Regent. If one could call noon morning. Jack was learning that noon was morning to an aristocrat.

Dressed in his formal Hussars uniform, Jack followed a liveried footman to the Prince Regent's private rooms. In the somewhat modest-looking library, the Prince Regent was wheeling around the chamber in a mechanical chair. Had the poor fellow gotten so fat he could no longer walk? It made sense that the human knees had not been constructed to support so heavy a load. Jack's gaze fell on the Regent's enormous stomach, which spread out so much it hid his thighs. The serving monarch was possessed of a fine face and a head of thick, reddish brown hair. "Good of you to come, Captain Dryden. I beg you forgive my tardiness, but my progress here was delayed."

Bowing before his monarch, Jack was, as he had been each time in the Regent's presence, inordinately flattered when the Prince Regent actually remembered his name. "How good it is to see you again, Your Royal Highness."

The Prince turned to a distinguished-looking man seated near him. This man with lightly grayed hair appeared to be perhaps a decade younger than the Prince Regent, which would make him about a decade older than Jack. "Have you met the Foreign Secretary, Lord Castlereagh?"

Jack's eyes widened. This prospective assignment must be very important. Lord Castlereagh was one of the most important men in all of England and certainly a man who worked closely with Jack's former commander in chief, the Duke of Wellington.

"I have not had that pleasure," Jack said, bowing now to the Foreign Secretary and hoping like hell he'd followed the proper procedure with his previous bow to the Prince.

The Prince eyed Jack. "I beg that you take a seat, my good man." He indicated a wood-framed camel chair beside the Foreign Secretary, and Jack did as bid.

"Before we begin," said the Prince, turning to Lord Castlereagh, "I must explain to you for further reference that Captain Dryden has just married Lord Sidworth's charming daughter, Lady Daphne, who everyone knows is the personification of discretion. Anything we tell this exemplary officer can be shared with Lady Daphne."

"With a woman?" a surprised Lord Castlereagh asked.

The Regent looked down his nose upon one of his highest ranking subjects. "Lady Daphne is not just a woman."

"Then I defer to your Royal Highness's judgment."

The chamber's very color scheme of brown, orange-reds, and greens and the solid masculinity of its furnishings invited a masculine gathering, Jack thought. With its restrained grandeur, the somber library seemed an appropriate place to discuss the crown's important work.

The Prince cleared his throat and began. "I received a communication from the newly created Field Marshall Wellington begging me to release you long enough to undertake one assignment for him. Since the duke assures me it's vital to the best interest of our country, I have agreed."

Jack's first thoughts were of Daphne. How long would it be before he once again beheld her, or once again held her?

Lord Castlereagh spoke next. "The Duke of Wellington and I have been in extensive communication on this grave issue we pray you can help resolve."

"I am completely at your service," Jack said.

The Foreign Secretary did not speak for a moment. "We're not altogether sure it is a situation you—or anyone—can resolve. It's actually very difficult to articulate, we know so little." He paused. "Did you perchance ever know a Captain Heffington?"

"Indeed," Jack said. "I worked with him on reconnaissance before Ciudad Rodrigo." His head lowered respectfully. "I heard that he died."

Lord Castlereagh nodded. "At the Siege of Sorauren a few weeks ago. He was supposed to be hurrying back to England with important information, but he just could not resist a good fight against the bloody French."

"A great pity," the Regent said, nodding.

Jack was inordinately curious to know what information poor old Heff had, but he would wait for his lordship to reveal it. "You are sure he possessed the information *before* the fateful battle?"

Lord Castlereagh nodded. "Yes. His batman was making arrangements for him to return to England when the battle interfered."

Jack was still wondering what information Heffington possessed that was so valuable.

The Foreign Secretary faced Jack. "You knew that Captain Heffington spoke French like a native?"

Jack nodded. "His mother, I believe, was French."

"That was the chief reason I recommended him for so important a mission."

What important mission?

"For some time I've been suspicious there was a leak somewhere in my office," Lord Castlereagh began.

"A leak?" Jack asked.

His lordship nodded. "I had cause to believe the enemy has breached the channels of communication between my office and our peninsular forces."

A most serious problem, to be sure, Jack thought. "You suspect someone on your staff?"

"It's not only possible, but probable. First, I suspected that some of my communiqués with Wellington may have been seen by someone who might be in the employ of the duc d'Arblier."

The very mention of the duc made Jack's blood boil. The Frenchman was as great a menace to England as that so-called French emperor he served. To Jack, he was a personal nemesis, and Jack would never feel either his country or his loved ones safe as long as the duc d'Arblier drew breath. How Jack would enjoy being the one to deprive him of that function!

"Acting completely alone in France," the Foreign Secretary continued, "Captain Heffington was able to learn the names of half a dozen high-ranking English officials who have been paid by the duc d'Arblier to betray their homeland. Since I could not risk such information getting into the wrong hands, I had requested that Captain Heffington impart that information in person to no one but me."

Jack knew how Captain Heffington worked. Not that he approved of it. Heffington wrote everything down—something Jack never practiced, never condoned. Jack preferred to keep important information in his head so the enemy could never get it. "You did not find that information on his body—or in his belongings after he died?"

The Foreign Secretary shook his head woefully. "You must see now why I said this is so bloody difficult. There was nothing on him, nothing in the personal effects in his tent."

Perhaps Jack *had* succeeded in imparting to old Heff the need to refrain from putting everything to pen and paper. "He may not have committed the information to paper."

"That is my fear."

Good lord, was Jack going to have to infiltrate back into France and try to duplicate the information? He spoke French, but certainly not like a native. His heart sank. Would he ever be able to make love to his very own wife?

"However," Lord Castlereagh added, "I have a suspicion—not really a suspicion founded upon anything solid, more of an optimistic hope—that when the captain received his mortal wound he may have given the vital information to one of his fellow officers."

"Have all of his fellow officers been questioned?" Jack asked.

The Foreign Secretary shrugged. "Not initially, no. You see, it wasn't until several days later that I even learned Heffington had not come straight back to England with his information, that he had died."

Blast that Heffington! He was a great patriot, but he sometimes did the most stupid things. "It was careless of the captain to have risked his life in battle before completing his assignment."

"Indeed it was! In fact, the entire chain of information was careless. Wellington was not informed when Heffington rejoined the camp, nor was I informed immediately when he died. Since then, Wellington and I have begun to piece all this together. By then, some of the soldiers in the siege had returned to England, others had died."

"Will his grace Wellington be able to give me full access to maps showing where all his troops were on the day of the battle?"

The Foreign Secretary nodded. "I took the liberty of anticipating your request, and Wellington's courier has just delivered me the information. The siege, as you probably know, lasted two days. Captain Heffington lost his life on the first day."

"Will I also have a list of which soldiers have either died or left camp since Sorauren?"

"I also anticipated that we would need that information." His lordship reached down and picked up several packets of dispatches. Jack had seen ones like that before. Dispatches entrusted only to the most trusted and capable couriers.

Jack took the packets. Now he had to pray that Heffington *had* written down his information. And passed it to someone else upon his death. If the corrupt English officials were not revealed, their kingdom could easily fall to the French.

One more thing crossed Jack's mind. "I will need your paymaster's lists of soldiers who were at the siege at Sorauren." Such a thought would likely never come to the Duke of Wellington, who thought all rank-and-file soldiers the scum of the earth. Like with Lord Castlereagh, it would never occur to Wellington that Heffington might pass such information to a common foot soldier.

"You will have that information tomorrow," Lord Castlereagh said.

Jack's last concern—and one he would *not* voice—was that the French duc had learned of Heffington's success and had seen that the captain was murdered before he could turn over the information, murdered in a battle that looked like a fair fight. That's the kind of devious deeds the vile Frenchman was capable of.

"It is our desire that no one in the government know you're working with us," the Prince said. "You will be free to work here in my library until. . ." He eyed the Foreign Secretary.

"Until Captain Dryden discovers what happened to Captain Heffington's important information," Lord Castlereagh answered.

The very future of England could be in Jack's hands. It had been weeks now since he had taken such pride in what he was doing.

He was so eager to begin his assignment, he only fleetingly thought of one very skinny, bespectacled lady with unruly hair.

$\mathcal{C}$hapter 3

Not having ever been in love before, Lady Daphne had no prior experience at being lovelorn. Even after she and her wonderful Jack had discovered they were in love, they had seen each other every day and therefore had no opportunity to dwell on the other's keenly felt absence.

But since the day of her wedding, Daphne had leisure to dwell on how acutely she missed Jack, to remember the feel of his lips on hers and the fluttering in her chest cavity when he hauled her into his strong arms, drawing her into him like clay to mold. She would recall the husky sound of his voice when he murmured endearments into her ear. She could almost feel his warm breath.

And she grew miserable. And irritable. She had snapped at Mama's maid merely because she offered to dress Daphne's hair. She refused to dine at the table with her parents and the sisters who remained at home. She had no desire to be submitted to their pitying stares. She had even tossed her poor cat out of her room merely because he wished to curl up on her lap and purr.

No contentment would ever be possible for Daphne until Jack returned.

Though only God—and the Prince Regent— knew where Jack was, she would sit before the desk in her bedchamber every day and write long epistles to him. Through her pen she could express sentiments that would seem hideously out of character coming from the lips of the former spinster Lady Daphne Chalmers. She would tell him how truly she loved him and how she never wanted to be separated from him again. She would look to their future together and share her hopes that they would have children, especially a little boy who would look like his father (but whom she prayed would not inherit his mother's deficient vision). She would admonish Jack not to take any risks with his person. Now that they were married, she wrote in the letters she was not sure she would ever have the courage to send, he must consider her feelings, he must not jeopardize his life and limb "for I am quite certain I would perish if something ever took you away from me."

When she read those words, she was astonished that she was capable of writing such insipid, flowery words. Then she would think of Jack, and her heart turned to the texture of warm butter.

While she was sitting at her desk the fourth day of Jack's absence, her duchess sister, Cornelia, quietly entered her bedchamber. Daphne gathered up the pages of her letter and shoved them into the drawer, then turned to face Cornelia. She looked over her sister's shoulder, searching for Cornelia's twin, Virginia. The two never went anywhere without each other. "Pray, where is Virginia?" Daphne asked.

Cornelia slung herself on Daphne's tester bed. "I am sure I don't know."

"But I thought you never went anywhere without your twin."

"If you must know, I did not want to be with her today."

Now this was a novel situation. The twins might not always agree—in fact, they often disagreed—but they were entirely too fond of one another to ever be truly out of charity with the other. Daphne's brows lowered. "Are you having a spat?"

"No!" Cornelia snapped.

"Then, pray, why did you come alone?"

"Really, Daf, Virginia and I are *not* inseparable. We have full lives apart from one another."

That was partially true. For all their closeness, the twins were vastly different. But Daphne had the intractable feeling that Cornelia had deliberately come without Virginia today for a particular reason.

And Daphne meant to find out what that was. "I can read you like a Minerva novel, pet. Why is it you've left Virginia behind today?"

Cornelia burst into tears.

Daphne rushed to her. "Whatever is the matter? It can't be that bad."

Cornelia buried her face into the velvet coverlet on Daphne's bed, her shoulders heaving with the force of her cries.

"Dearest, you must tell me what's wrong." Daphne gentled her voice and stroked Cornelia's thin shoulders. She was the petite twin.

"I'm in the most horrid trouble."

"Surely it can't be that bad."

Sniff. Sniff. "It's worse than bad."

Daphne fetched a lace-trimmed hanky and offered it to her sister. "Perhaps I can help. You must tell me."

Cornelia sat up and blotted at her tear-streaked face, sniffed, and met Daphne's concerned gaze.

"If I tell you, you must promise never to reveal to Virginia what I'm about to say."

This was another novel experience. The twins shared every confidence. They had for their entire three and twenty years. "Are you sure that's what you want?"

"Yes, I am most decidedly sure."

"Very well. I will honor your request. I will never tell Virginia—unless you give me leave to do so."

Cornelia blew her nose and eyed Daphne. "I am in a most horrid predicament, and I can't let Lankersham ever learn of my dual discretions."

Her infidelities. Was that all? Daphne had always known about Cornelia's infidelities, and she suspected Lankersham did, too. "Well, of course, that simply isn't done. One does not tell one's husband about one's lovers."

"Oh, it's even worse than that!"

That Cornelia had multiple lovers, Daphne also knew. "Then Lankersham has found out?"

Cornelia shook her head. "It's not that, either."

"Then what can have distressed you so?"

"I feel it's so terribly hopeless. If only your captain were here. I know he could help me."

Daphne's family had learned of Jack's cleverness that extricated Wellington from all manner of hopeless situations, but Daphne was a bit miffed over this praise. After all, she had been just as instrumental in saving the Regent's life as Jack.

She stiffened and gave the duchess a haughty stare. "I assure you, with the exception of sword fighting, I am just as capable as Captain Dryden."

"That's why I'm here."

The two sisters stared at one another, and Cornelia's eyes filled with tears again.

Daphne drew her close, hugging her. "It can't be that bad, my dear love."

Cornelia whimpered. "It is."

Would Cornelia ever get to the point? "You must tell me all about it. I might be able to help."

"I've been paying exorbitant sums to a blackmailer to keep him from giving Lankersham love letters I wrote to Major Styles."

So that explained why not just one problem plagued Cornelia, but two. She was not only trying to keep the letters away from her husband, but she was also getting deeply into debt in order to prevent the letters from reaching Lankersham.

"Have you been forced to go to the money lenders?"

Cornelia nodded ruefully.

"This is a very grave situation, indeed, but cheer up, my sweet! You've come to the right person. I shall investigate the matter for you. I will find out who this vile person is, and I will recover your letters."

Ever since the business with the threats on the Regent's life, Daphne had fancied herself to be most clever at discreet inquiries. She would show Jack! He wasn't to be the only clever investigator in their family.

"How can you be so very confident?"

Daphne shrugged. "I supposed it comes with being the firstborn."

"You've always been bossy, but until you met Captain Dryden I never knew you to be particularly clever about investigating."

"It's a latent talent I've discovered. Now, you must tell me everything. I seem to have a vague memory of a flirtation between you and some military officer, but was that not a couple of years ago?"

"Indeed it was." Cornelia's tears threatened again. "He's dead now."

"Your major?" The thought of a dead major was too similar to dead a captain, and such a thought made Daphne feel as if she'd stopped a cannonball. Dear God, she thought, Jack has to be safe.

Cornelia nodded. "He died just weeks ago."

"Is that when the blackmail commenced?"

"Yes."

Obviously, someone got the major's letters from his personal effects after he died. But who? "Was there a . . . Mrs. Styles?"

"Yes." Cornelia looked up, her face suddenly bright. "It must be her! She has reason to loathe me, to want to ruin me."

"And she could probably use the money."

Cornelia's eyes narrowed. "She could live exceedingly well off the money she's drained from me."

"Do you have the blackmail letter still?"

"It wasn't just one letter. I received the first about ten days ago, and I paid. Then yesterday, I received another letter, demanding even more money than the first." She reached into her reticule, withdrew the folded letter, and handed it to her elder sister.

Daphne studied it, not just the few words that had been printed, but she noted that it was written on high-quality parchment. It read:

Leave £1,000 in a bag on the Penzance mail post Thursday & your letters will be returned.

"It's obvious the person who wrote this printed to disguise his or her distinctive hand," Daphne said. "This person is possessed of a bold hand."

"Well, of course she's bold!"

"Don't jump to conclusions. We don't know for sure the letter writer is Mrs. Styles. Tell me, how was the letter delivered?"

"By the post."

"From London?"

Cornelia nodded.

"Just as I expected."

"I would have thought the person might be in Penzance."

Daphne shook her head. "No. Because Penzance is so far from London and there are so many stops between the two cities, our blackmailer knew there would be many bags on the coach. He—or she—could easily remove one without it being missed. I wouldn't be surprised if the person was able to remove it before the coach ever left London. Was the first payment also placed on the Penzance mail coach?"

"No, it was on the Edinburough coach."

Another vast distance from London. "Did you deliver it to the post chaise?"

Cornelia looked down her dainty nose at Daphne. "A duchess doesn't go near so common a conveyance."

"Then you had one of your servants deliver it?"

"My maid."

"Did you ask her to watch after it?"

"I never thought to. I assumed someone in Edinborough would pick it up."

"It's a very good thing you've come to me. You are much too simple-minded to deal with something like this."

"That's a wicked thing to say about me!"

"But you've got so many other fine attributes. No one in London can match you for exquisite taste in clothing—and you must own, the sons you bore are not at all simple minded. They are brilliant little fellows, which I don't mind saying, even though they are my own nephews."

Cornelia studied Daphne from beneath lowered brows. "You only say that because dear little Bexley is so much like you. Everyone says he's clever like his aunt."

"Comfort yourself with the realization I'm the clever sister because you got the beauty. Which would you rather have had bestowed upon you?"

The dainty duchess of the huge brown eyes gave her sister a smirk. "The beauty, of course."

And Daphne was happy she received the brains. "We've got three days to try and discover the blackmailer's identity before Thursday."

"But if you don't succeed. . . I cannot possibly come up with a thousand pounds in just three days."

"Oh, there's no question about it. You'd have to return to the moneylenders. I understand they are only too happy to give financial assistance to a duchess. They know Lankersham's vastly wealthy."

"He's already been so generous to me, I can't possibly ask for more."

"Especially not an excessive amount like that." Daphne recalled that Jack accounted for all his needs on a mere hundred pounds a year. "It seems to me the way to trap your blackmailer would be to select your strongest footmen, install them in the same livery as the post chaise men wear, put them on the coach bound for Penzance, and have them apprehend the person who snatches the bag."

"I'm afraid Lankersham would notice the absence of our strongest footmen."

"You can concoct some story to explain their departure." After all, Cornelia was adept at concealing her little romances from her husband. "First, though, you must procure the post livery and make sure you have it by Thursday."

"Would I have to put real money into the bag?"

"You might have to. The blackmailer may be watching you. He's got to know to get your hands on that much money you would have to go to Jews." Daphne spun around and glared at her sister. "Don't tell me you sent your maid to the moneylenders for you?"

"Of course I did! A duchess can't go traipsing about in The City, mingling with *that* sort of person."

"This time, *you* will go. And I shall accompany you."

"I certainly hope you don't go ordering around your captain like you do your sisters!"

"Speaking of sisters, why can we not share your . . . your perplexing predicament with Virginia?"

"Because she's so utterly, disgustingly besotted over that husband of hers. She does not approve of my little flirtations, and she'd probably have apoplexy if she knew I'd written passionate love letters to Major Styles. Honestly, Daphne, I'm sick to death of her praises over her Sir Ronald."

It would have been nice, Daphne thought, if Cornelia was possessed of a bit more devotion toward the duke she had married. Daphne could not remember Cornelia ever praising a single thing about poor Lankersham.

Daphne herself was perplexed that Cornelia could have written *passionate* letters to a married major. She certainly hoped Jack never found out about them because he loathed adultery. She smiled to herself as she thought about the man she had married.

"We shall go to the moneylenders on Wednesday," Daphne said. In the meantime, she had some inquiries to make.

* * *

Damn but his back ached. Jack had spent more than twelve hours a day each of the past two days slumped over the dispatches in the Regent's private library in Brighton. He knew the position of every officer who fought at Sorauren. And since obtaining the paymaster's report, he had the names of all soldiers who had served there under Wellington's command. It had gotten to where Jack had memorized the names of most of those who had been at the siege. It had been arduous work.

As foolhardy as Heffington had been to jump into the fight when he had not completed his previous assignment, Jack could not help but to admire the man's courage. According to the plans Wellington had forwarded to Lord Castlereagh, Heffington led a charge at the very front—a most dangerous position, to be sure.

From the information Jack possessed, it was impossible to tell what had happened with Heffington's list.

If there was a physical list.

As much as it pained him to admit it, Jack could proceed no further without returning to the Peninsula.

His stomach knotted. He couldn't go off on a long voyage like that without seeing Daphne. And he couldn't see her without telling her what he was working on. That's how it was with him and Daphne. They shared everything.

And it wasn't as if she would go around blabbering about his duties. Everyone knew how discreet she could be.

There was nothing for it but to beg the Regent's permission to explain to Daphne—face to face— that he had to return to the Peninsula.

He had to see her.

His work had kept him so occupied that he hadn't been plagued with thoughts of her as he had during those four days when he'd had nothing to do except wait.

But his nights were sheer torture, lying there longing for his slender Daphne, dreaming of the night she would become his well-loved wife.

Before he asked the Regent's permission to visit Daphne, he drafted a letter to the Foreign Secretary requesting him to arrange for the necessary preparations for Jack to return to Spain. He gave the letter to the Regent's special courier, then begged permission to speak with the Regent.

* * *

Hatchments were on the windows at the Styles' House on Edgeware Road. Daphne knew she should be ashamed of herself—a perfect stranger—for intruding on the widow's grief, but she had a duty to her own sister to uncover the identity of the vile creature who was blackmailing her.

She had thought her visit would be more well received were she to arrive in the Earl of

Sidworth's crested coach. Those not born to the aristocracy (except for Jack) were impressed over things like that. She waited in the coach while her father's tiger presented her card at the door of the fairly modest house.

A pretty young woman in black personally answered the door, and flicked her gaze out toward the street upon reading the card, then nodded to the tiger, who had been instructed to ask if his mistress could pay her respects.

A moment later, Daphne sat in the drawing room with Mrs. Styles. "So kind of you to allow me to call," Daphne began. "While we've never met, I felt it my duty to come and offer you my condolences, seeing as how our husbands served together in the Peninsula."

"That is very kind of you. Did you know my husband?"

Daphne could not lie. "No." Well, maybe a little lie. . . "But my dear Jack often spoke of him."

The petite brunette offered a wan smile. "He was always popular. And handsome, too."

"Though I hadn't met him, I had seen him before. He *was* very handsome." She needn't tell the poor widow she had seen her husband dancing attendance on her own sister at Almack's.

Mrs. Styles smiled again, a distant look upon her face. "One feels so alone---" She faltered. She was probably the same age as Daphne, but in her frail state she seemed younger and more vulnerable. Daphne's heart went out to her. The poor woman was obviously suffering over the loss of her husband. Which was completely understandable. How grateful Daphne was to the Regent for assigning Jack to his own regiment so Jack would not have to return to the Peninsula.

She studied the pitiable widow. Like Cornelia, she was petite. She also was possessed of dark eyes and dark hair. Like Cornelia. The major certainly ran true to form in his taste in women.

Daphne wondered if the widow knew of her husband's affair with the Duchess of Lankersham. If she were the blackmailer, of course, she would.

Since Daphne was coming to understand about the mental state of a woman in love (owing to her feelings for her very own Jack), she was confident she would be able to gauge the woman's reaction to a mention of the duchess. But she was not yet ready to spring that upon the lady. First she must establish a comforting presence with the widow. "Of course. How unnatural it would be if you did not feel alone now. Were you and the major married long?"

"Seven years."

"You must have been quite the child bride."

Mrs. Styles offered Daphne a faint smile. "I was seventeen, and my George was one and twenty when we wed."

"Do you have children?"

There was affection in her voice and pride flashing in Mrs. Styles' eyes. "Our son is at school, and the baby—our daughter—is napping."

"Then you've been blessed in other ways."

"Indeed."

Daphne gazed around the room. If Mrs. Styles had recently come into a great deal of money from committing vile deeds such as blackmail, there was certainly no sign of it here. The faded green brocade on the sofa had worn so thin in places that the stuffing showed through.

From the way she crossed her legs at the ankle, Daphne could observe that the soles on the widow's shoes, too, had worn so thin a small hole revealed her black stockings.

Now, Daphne would throw the first gauntlet. "My sister, the Duchess of Lankersham, has two little boys. I have discovered the joy of little boys. I'd never been around little fellows much before, owing to the fact there were nothing but girls—six of us—in my family."

The woman did not register the slightest sign of recognition at the mention of Cornelia. "Your father must be a happy grandfather, then, finally to have little boys."

Daphne gave her a warm smile. "Indeed he is, and he's unbearably indulgent toward the little rascals."

"My only comfort after my loss is that my father is excessively fond of my son and will step in to help me with him."

Did she mean financially? Or was that implication to be a ruse for the purpose of covering up new-found wealth? "Having a man to help guide them will indeed be a great comfort. Is your father in London?"

She shook her head. "But he's not far away. He's in Middlesex."

Daphne wondered if Mrs. Styles' father, like her own, had no sons of his own. "Did your father have only daughters, too?"

The lady nodded. "In fact, I am his only child. He's been after me to move back home, and I believe I will. It will be good for my little boy, and to be perfectly honest with you, I don't know how much longer I can afford to live in London."

"I'm so sorry."

"A widow's portion is so much less than what one has when one's husband is able to generate an income."

Daphne was convinced of the woman's sincerity, convinced she knew nothing of her husband's affair.

As she took her leave, she prayed that Mrs. Styles would never learn of her husband's adultery.

Later that afternoon as Daphne was returning to Sidworth House and saw Jack's Warrior tethered in front, her heartbeat roared. She nearly leaped from the moving carriage in her haste to see her husband.

$\mathcal{C}$ hapter 4

She could tell from the considerable lather on Jack's horse that he hadn't been there long—and he'd obviously ridden a long distance. Thrilled almost beyond endurance, she raced up the steps and threw open the door to her parents' home.

Daphne hurried up the marble stairway and burst into the drawing room where Lady Sidworth and her youngest daughter, Rosemary, sat upon a silken French sofa speaking to Jack. At first all Daphne saw was the back of his dark head. He turned, saw her, and immediately got to his feet. He wore his regimentals and was still the most handsome officer in the kingdom.

Their eyes met. Her heart stampeded, and she launched herself into his arms. She stood there in the shelter of his powerful arms, glorying in the feel of being held by this man she loved so thoroughly.

Far too soon for her liking, he placed her an arm's length away and lowered his brows. Why would he be out of charity with her? "Your mother was just inquiring about my recent indisposition."

Uh oh. Poor Jack had not have been apprised of what his particular indisposition was. The pity of it was, Daphne would be hard pressed to remember if she had attributed his infirmity to measles or to mumps. She always got those two mixed up, both beginning with the letter M and both being common contagious diseases she had never contracted. Which one was it that had caused that poor boy at Eton with Papa to be carried off dead?

Oh, dear. What was she to do? Change the subject of course! She turned a bright face to him. "How well you have recovered, my dearest! You look the very picture of health."

"Frankly," Lady Sidworth said, climbing from her seat, crossing the room, and squinting into Jack's face as if it were a portrait hanging at the Royal Gallery, "I'm astonished you've recovered so quickly. And so completely."

"The surgeon was equally astonished at how quickly Jack recovered from musket ball wounds back in the Peninsula," Daphne babbled. She had no idea if there was a morsel of truth in what she was saying, but she hoped to turn the conversation away from his recent infirmity.

The idea of Jack's body stopping a musket ball almost sent Lady Sidworth into apoplexy. Her hands clasped at her heart, and her chin dropped, mouth open. "A musket ball! How was your poor mother to bear it?"

Daphne cocked her head and peered at her mother as if she had completely taken leave of her senses. "Mrs. Dryden wasn't the one suffering; it was my poor Jack!" Of course, Daphne still had no idea if Jack had ever stopped a musket ball, but the story was proving to be a nice diversion.

"That's enough, Daphne." Jack's voice was stern.

"What is my daughter getting you into now?"

They all turned as Lord Sidworth strolled into the room and shook hands with Jack. "Good to see you, Captain."

Daphne stood back and glowed. It was impossible for her father to conceal the great affection he held for Jack. Much more so than with his other sons-in-law, the Duke of Lankersham and Sir Ronald Johnson, not that both of them weren't perfect dears. They just weren't as handsome or as brilliant or as brave or as out-and-out good as Jack.

"Well, Mother," the earl said to his wife, "it looks like you're finally going to have let our Daphne go."

Jack cleared his throat. "Though I am greatly looking forward to making my home with Lady Daphne, she may need to stay here a bit longer. I beg the opportunity to have a few private words with my wife."

Daphne felt as if she'd fallen from high in the clouds. She linked her arm through Jack's. "It's been an age since we saw one another. Do allow us some privacy."

"Come on, Mother." The earl began to lead his wife and youngest daughter from the chamber.

Jack beamed down at her. "I was going to suggest we take a walk."

"You've taken the very words from my mouth."

* * *

A few minutes later they were strolling the paths of Green Park. God, but he wanted to kiss her! And he damned well did not want to have to leave her. Nor did he want to tell her he had to return to Spain. But he could not allow her to get her hopes up.

"I missed you terribly," she said.

He smiled and squeezed her hand. "Not as much as I missed you. You, at least, had diversions and familiar company."

"Are you at liberty to tell me where you went?"

"I am. Now." Most women would have demanded an explanation. His Daphne, thank God, wasn't like most women. Perhaps that was why they got along so well. She thought rather like a man, though she was most definitely a woman. A woman he desired more than he ever thought possible. He allowed himself the luxury of remembering the feel of holding her slender body against his. He drew in a breath and gazed down at her. "I've been in Brighton."

"At the Royal Pavilion?"

He nodded.

"No doubt the Regent had need of your superior sleuthing skills."

"*Superior*? Is that not one of those words I forbid you to use when describing me?"

"I know, dearest. It's beastly difficult to describe you without using those kinds of words. You *are* quite the best at all you do. And it *is* just the two of us." She looked up at him, rather adoringly, he thought with satisfaction. He took her hand and kissed it.

"As it was, the Regent was the liaison between Lord Castlereagh and me."

Behind the spectacles, her pretty green eyes widened with astonishment. "The Foreign Secretary?"

"Yes."

"I'm well acquainted with his wife. She's one of the patronesses at Almack's, but he doesn't often come to the assemblies. I understand he stays terribly busy."

"I can well believe it."

"Can you tell me the nature of what problem he laid in your lap?"

He chuckled. "What makes you think the most important people in government would need my help?"

"A woman's intuition."

"As it happens, I have been on an assignment for the Foreign Secretary and the peninsular commander."

"The new Duke of Wellington?"

He nodded.

"And now you have solved the problem!"

He drew in a breath. "I did not. It was impossible for me to glean the necessary information from a distance of several hundred miles."

Her brows lowered, her spectacles slipped farther down toward the tip of her nose. "I don't think I'm going to like what you're about to say next."

Lord and Lady Sidworth did not raise a stupid daughter. He nodded ruefully. "I'm afraid I must go to Spain, but it will be a very short trip."

"You could be killed!"

"My dearest Daphne, I could be killed by a footpad right here in London."

She pouted. "I don't like to talk about you being killed. Just this morning I spoke with a Peninsular widow, and I told myself I would die if I ever lost you." Her face was ravaged with pain when she looked up at him. "And I would."

"I feel the very same about you, my sweet, and I promise to hurry back to you."

"No, you don't, Captain Dryden! You will not go to the Peninsula without me."

Their eyes locked and held.

Good lord! Was she thinking the same thing he was thinking?

He was almost robbed of breath. Both stilled. They drew closer. He possessed just barely enough self control *not* to pull her into his arms.

But not enough to deny what she was offering.

Suddenly the prospect of bringing his wife to Spain held great allure. "You could be killed."

She giggled.

"Very well, my vixen. I'm to be in Portsmouth tomorrow morning."

She squeezed both his hands. "It shall be a grand honeymoon."

$\mathcal{C}$hapter 5

Daphne promised her husband she would be ready to depart for Portsmouth in a little over an hour. Selecting clothing for the journey was not the sort of thing she applied her energies to. One dress was the same as another to her. And she had been told her wardrobe was now exemplary since Mama had put Cornelia in command of her wedding trousseau.

Only one matter pressed on her as she prepared to depart for Spain. She needed to tell Cornelia she would not be able to accompany her to the money lenders. In her note, she urged the duchess to take Virginia into her confidence and suggested those two sisters go together. "I am sorry, pet, that I must leave," she wrote in conclusion. "If you have not extricated yourself from this problem by the time I return, I vow to help you then."

For the journey to Portsmouth, Lord Sidworth insisted the newlyweds take his luxurious coach.

"I don't know how I can bear allowing my first little girl to go off across the ocean." Lady Sidworth clutched at her heart. "What if the ship sinks?"

Daphne's pragmatic father stepped up and put a reassuring hand at his wife's shoulder. "She's only going to be gone for a few weeks, and the

Royal Navy has provided one of its finest frigates to take our distinguished son to Wellington."

That her father had referred to Jack as his son melted Daphne's heart.

As the new Captain and Mrs. Dryden departed, Papa pressed a bottle of his favorite port into Jack's hands. Mama had Cook present the wedding couple with a basket brimming with food for the journey.

For someone who had never been farther north than Derbyshire or farther south than Brighton, Daphne was thrilled to be going to sunny Spain. And on an ocean vessel! What a grand adventure awaited her.

She settled back into the squabs beside her husband and bid a cheery farewell to her family as they rode off into the London twilight.

Once her family was no longer within view, Jack drew her to him, and they tenderly kissed.

"Dearest?" she asked.

"Yes, my love?"

"When do we arrive in Portsmouth?"

He frowned. "Tomorrow morning. Just in time to board the ship before it sails."

"When will we have our wedding night?"

His sultry eyes met hers. He did not respond for a moment. "I have requested that we have a private chamber on the ship. Tomorrow night."

She knew how difficult it was for him to wait. After all, he was a man. And men did have lusty . . . needs. "Do you think it's something that could be managed in a . . . carriage?" She hated to admit how ignorant she was of such matters.

He did not respond for a moment. She thought maybe that male anatomy thing might be at work. "It could," he finally said. "But we're not."

"Why? I am your wife!"

"My dearest wife, while it is something that experienced couples could manage, it is not the way I plan to make love to my very own, beloved wife the first time."

Jack always considered others over himself. It was one of the things she loved about the honorable man she had married.

Snuggling close to him, she settled her head into his chest, basking in the comforting warmth of their love, in the feel of his muscled arm pressing her close to him. Soon the environs of London were behind them, and the carriage grew dark. The only lights were the buttery glow of lanterns on passing coaches.

"Are you ready now to tell me why you must return to Spain?" she finally asked.

He told her about Heffington's mission and the man's subsequent death before he could get the information to Lord Castlereagh.

"Was Heffington married?" she asked.

"What does that have to do with anything?"

"Silly. He could have imparted the information to his wife."

"No spy would *ever* take a woman into his confidence—unless, of course, that woman was Lady Daphne. Besides, Heffington was a bachelor."

"How nicely you got yourself out of hot water, Captain! I am happy to hear there was no Mrs. Heffington for I would have gotten excessively blue-deviled to think of his poor wife's great loss."

Her husband squeezed her shoulder and pressed soft kisses into her hair.

"So now you must actually communicate in person with other officers who served beside Captain Heffington on the day of his death?"

"It's my only hope, and it's a very slim one. Assuming that Heffington *did* pass off that information, why wouldn't the person who possessed that information have turned it over to the Foreign Office by now?"

"Obviously he would, if he knew the significance of the list."

"It is possible the person he passed it to did not know its importance. Heffington may have drawn his last breath before he could communicate with the other man."

"It seems to me," she said, "this is very much like searching for a needle in a ."

"Indeed it is." Jack held her close but was disturbingly quiet.

Then she heard a soft snore.

She remembered he'd not slept the previous night as he hurried to London to see her before he went to Spain.

She smiled to herself. One day they could tell their grandchildren about this exciting honeymoon aboard a Royal Navy ship hastening to the Peninsula.

* * *

Excitement coursed through her as she and Jack strolled onto the frigate, the HMS *Avalon*. The captain greeted them as if Jack were the Prince Regent himself. "We've held up sailing," he told them. "Lord Castlereagh's orders were that nothing take precedence over getting Captain Dryden and his wife to Spain as quickly as possible."

Jack's gaze had scanned the fleet, three-masted frigate. "I'm sorry we've delayed you. It's a fine ship you've got here. How many guns?"

"Twenty four. I'll show you around once we've pushed off. Allow me to show you two to your quarters now."

"And the winds?" Jack asked.

Captain St. James smiled. "Most favorable."

He took them below deck to the bow of the ship where the captain's own private chamber was located. "It's such a short trip, I'll just bunk with my first officer. Lord Castlereagh was most insistent that you and your bride have the finest chamber on the ship."

"I am indebted to you," Jack said, shaking the man's hand as he left them.

Daphne was surprised that her valise had already been placed in the chamber. "Oh look, my dearest, we shall have our own window! What a wonderful cabin!"

He came to stand behind her, his hand touching her waist, his head resting on her shoulder. She felt the heat of him and drew in his musky male scent. They watched in comforting silence as the ship set sail, sweeping away from the harbor that was home to the British fleet. Landward, on a bluff overlooking the nearly round harbor, Portchester Castle guarded England's seagoing pride, its rounded gray bricks unchanged over the centuries of the millennium. With a war going on, the nearly vacant harbor was strangely sleepy now.

She marveled at the vastness of the mesmerizing water stretching out beyond the harbor, then peered back. The shoreline buildings diminished as their ship sailed into the open sea.

What a wonder it was to be on a ship! Her first ocean voyage.

Her glance fell to the slender bed.

And her heartbeat quickened.

She became acutely cognizant of the intimacy of standing in this small chamber, alone with a man. A man who was now her husband. She thought of the words the clergyman had spoken during their wedding ceremony, *and your two bodies shall become one*. Her breath felt thin. Her pulse accelerated. "Dearest?"

Jack settled his big, sturdy hands on her shoulders. "Yes?"

"Does a wedding night have to be at night?"

He burst out laughing, then he grew serious. His voice was husky, his eyes smoldering as he said, "Not necessarily."

He drew her into his embrace and hungrily kissed her.

She knew she was going to adore being married. She did not object in the least when she felt his palm cup the little swell of bosom she possessed. Her breath seemed to swish from her lungs, and the room became excessively hot. Whatever it was he was doing to her, she did not want it to stop.

Then the ship pitched up and down, batting them into the wooden wall. Jack never let go of his firm hold on her. The ship continued pitching them as if they were corks bobbing upon waves. Jack scooped her into his arms and carried her to the bed.

She suddenly felt the contents of her stomach churning. Then rising. Sweat beaded on her brow. *Uh oh.* She was going to retch.

"Are you all right?" Jack murmured, studying her face with concern.

"I. Don't. Think. I. Am."

"Do you need a chamber pot?"

That was exactly what she needed! All she could do was nod. A sloshing in her stomach began to rise.

He had barely set the pot in front of her when she began to violently retch. While her brain was registering how truly horrid she felt, the misery was doubly compounded by how vastly embarrassed she was over her disgusting action, right in front of Jack. How could any man be attracted to a woman who retched practically in his lap? She was mortified.

And she could not remember ever feeling worse.

Her brow was wet. Her hair was damp. And chills racked her body.

Even though Jack had to be disgusted over her display, he betrayed no sign of it. He stroked her forehead and spoke softly. "Are you better now?"

She shook her head. "Is there anything one can do to keep this boat . . . level?"

He shook his head. "I'm afraid not. It appears my poor wife is suffering from sea sickness."

It had never—not even as she was casting up her accounts—occurred to her that she could be sea sick. It was some small relief to know that she had not contracted some fatal disease. She'd felt so wretched, she had thought perhaps she might be dying. "How long will it last?"

He shrugged. "Sometimes it can last the entire voyage."

A lone tear dripped along her face.

"I'm so sorry, love," he murmured.

How could he stand to be near her? She was completely humiliated. "I am so embarrassed."

He drew her into his arms and held her close. "There's nothing to be embarrassed over. If I'd had any idea you would be affected like this, I'd never have allowed you to come."

"Does this wretchedness go away when one gets on shore?"

"Indeed it does."

"How much longer before we reach Spain?"

"No one ever knows. It depends on the winds. With luck, we'll be there tomorrow. Sometimes, though, the winds can keep a ship in a small area of water for days on end."

"I may have to kill myself."

"Not while I draw breath."

She would much have preferred to suffer alone, but he refused to leave her side. At first she had been embarrassed to look up into his worried face after her violent retching, but as the agonizing hours mounted, acceptance replaced embarrassment. She felt so utterly wretched, she fleetingly thought death would be preferable to remaining on this ship.

She lost all sense of time. The only thing she was sure of—besides her complete misery—was that Jack never stopped hovering over her, murmuring comforting words and wiping her beaded brow with cloths soaked in cool water.

* * *

He refused to leave her side during the miserable crossing. He thanked God that over the past few years the British had driven the French almost back to their homeland, which meant the British troops no longer had to journey all the way down to Portugal as they had when he'd first gone to the Peninsula.

Now they could come to Spain from the Bay of Biscay—a much closer route. He prayed for a quick voyage.

She would awaken and retch, express her embarrassment, then collapse back into the bed. "Are you certain I'm not dying?" she would croak.

He would assure her as he smoothed her damp brow, cover her, then kiss her cheek.

"I'm so sorry I'm spoiling your wedding night."

"We have a lifetime of shared nights ahead. One or two days' difference does not signify."

It was dawn the next day when the frigate sailed into the tiny port in northern Spain.

"You'll be better when I get you off this blasted boat," Jack said. He stood over her in the dark room, tenderly stroking her face with a single finger. Then he bent to pick her up as if she weighed no more than a loaf of bread.

"What are you doing?" she asked.

"I'm carrying you off this damned boat. You're too weak to walk." His voice softened. "I could draw and quarter myself for bringing you here."

She set a gentle hand to his cheek. "Don't blame yourself, dearest. I'm the one who insisted on coming. I daresay I'll be right as rain as soon as I'm on steady ground."

"I pray that you are."

Captain St. James told Jack to hurry back from his mission because he had been instructed to keep the ship in harbor until they returned. "And as valuable as I'm told your mission is," St. James said, "I'd rather be chasing the French."

Daphne gave him a bleary eyed glare. "I'd rather you be doing that as well."

Jack knew the Royal Navy needed every vessel. He made a silent vow to work with great speed.

"Dearest?" Daphne asked.

"Yes?"

"It is not possible to return to England by land, is it?"

He squeezed her hand and smiled. "Unfortunately, no."

As they were disembarking, his gaze scanned along the quay where dark-skinned Basques in white shirts were loading crates of oranges onto the British ship. Donkeys laden with goods trotted along the narrow streets of this busy little port city. And above the smaller locals who were going about their daily business, Jack could see a tall man dressed in the distinctive uniform of a British army officer. He was too far away to recognize, but Jack could tell he was gazing at them.

To his profound relief, once Daphne was on solid ground, she recovered remarkably. He hated like the devil that she had no time to rest, to try to get back her strength—and her appetite—but the Duke of Wellington's aide-de-camp, Lieutenant-Colonel John Freemantle, met them as soon as they cleared the ship and informed them they would depart immediately.

It had taken Jack a second to remember who in the blazes was the Duke of Wellington. For too long now Jack had known the general as Lord Wellesley, Commander in Chief of Peninsular Forces. But now, since their spectacular victory at Vitoria, their capable leader had been elevated to the Duke of Wellington.

That was one of the things Jack disliked most about titles. People were forever discarding perfectly acceptable, highly recognizable names in order to adopt a new moniker no one would easily recognize for some time.

Lord Sidworth had suggested Jack allow the Prince Regent to bestow the title Viscount Lindon upon Jack. Jack could not imagine any reason that could compel him to participate in such nonsensical name jockeying. He'd been Jack Dryden since the day he was born. He was proud to be known as Jack Dryden. He liked to think the name Jack Dryden had earned a certain amount of respect. So why would he want to change it?

"It will take several hours before we can reach the British camp," Freemantle said. "I've taken the liberty of procuring two horses for you. They look to be good beasts."

The pair of stallions were tethered only yards away, next to Freemantle's—which clearly belonged to a high-ranking officer. After they mounted, Jack eyed his bride and took pride in the fact Daphne sat a horse as well as any man.

As they left the port town of Gijon, Jack's thoughts flitted over the past several years the English had occupied this southern European peninsula. How it had changed since he had first arrived in Portugal back in '08 when all the northern Spanish ports were in French hands!

He hated to recall all those blazingly hot, barren Spanish battlefields upon which the British had so bravely fought. Now the British troops had advanced so far north they had reached the Pyrenees, pushing the stinking French back toward their homeland.

How the terrain, too, had changed in these five years, Jack reflected as the three of them rode over a much more verdant landscape than Jack had generally associated with Spain. Their current trail was shaded by thickets of pine and ornamented with towering cypress. Always, their path meandered near the lovely River Bidassod.

And always, Jack tensed with fear that his nemesis, the duc d'Arblier, was watching him from the surrounding hills, waiting to murder him as he had murdered Jack's best friend. Damn, but Jack missed Edwards. Over the course of five years of battle, Jack had seen a lot of death, but none had ever affected him as profoundly as Edwards'.

Too many times now Jack had defied d'Arblier's deathtraps, too many times he'd cheated death. God help him, he wanted to live. Now that he was married, more than ever.

For Daphne.

Late that afternoon, outside the village of Lesaca, they found the Duke of Wellington pacing the quaint little tree-shaded cemetery beside a lovely old Catholic church.

"Are our men buried there?" Jack asked Freemantle before the three of them dismounted.

"Oh, no. It's just that our camp headquarters is just on the other side of the graveyard, and his grace finds the cemetery a peaceful place where he can think."

Jack made eye contact with Freemantle. "I have in my possession a letter from the Prince Regent addressed to the duke. It was written to inform his grace that my wife, who is the embodiment of discretion, will be part of this investigation."

The other officer shrugged. "Then I expect both of you should come along to speak to the duke."

As the three of them drew nearer, Wellington stopped pacing and watched them. Because of his commanding presence, he seemed a much larger man that he actually was. It always surprised Jack that his commander was at least a half of a foot shorter than Jack's six feet, two inches. The duke wore a uniform but had left off his hat and medals. Though he was past forty, his hair was free from gray, and his waist free from fat. Jack hoped he would look like that a decade from now when he was that age.

"Good of you to come, Captain Dryden," Wellington said, hitching a brow as he eyed Daphne.

"Allow me to present my wife, your grace. Lady Daphne." As Daphne curtsied and spoke prettily, Jack handed the duke the letter bearing the seal of the Prince Regent. "This letter from the Regent will explain that my wife is to be included in all aspects of this inquiry."

The duke broke the seal, then ran his eye over the letter, nodding. When he was finished, he offered Daphne a weak smile before turning to his aide-de-damp. "You are dismissed, Freemantle."

After the aide-de-camp took his leave, the duke said, "Pray, Captain and Lady Daphne, come walk with me."

Falling into step beside Wellington, Jack was flattered that the Commander in Chief of the entire peninsular army always remembered him.

"I understand you're now with the Guards," Wellington said to him.

"Yes, your grace. It was not a transfer I would have chosen." It was a nice and safe assignment to the Regent's regiment in the Capital, an assignment the Regent ordered to please Daphne.

Wellington nodded. "But, alas, one has no free choice when the monarch himself orders one about."

"Precisely, your grace."

"I know well of what I speak. I wanted you back in Spain, but it seems the Regent has decided he wants you at his own beck and call."

"He did allow me to come here."

"Because he knew he'd get you back as soon as you complete this assignment! But that's enough of that. Now, this nasty business about Heffington . . . I'm destitute of words to describe my anger when I found out he'd entered camp and not apprised me of the information he'd discovered. Then the fool officer had the poor judgment to get himself killed! What a terrible disservice he's done to Britain!"

Jack was sure that had not been Heff's intent, but he was not about to disagree with the duke. "A beastly business, to be sure."

"You must tell me how I can assist you." Wellington turned to Daphne. "And Lady Daphne."

"The reason I'm here, your grace," Jack said, "is to be able to interview those men who fought near Heffington on the day of his death. I hold a slim hope that Captain Heffington passed on the list before he died. Unfortunately, that's our only hope at present."

"Then it's my profound hope you're successful."

"I thank you for seeing that such very fine records of troop positions were kept. I now know by heart the names of every officer and every foot soldier who was within a hundred yards of Heffington at Sorauren at the time he was hit."

The duke nodded. "Then you merely need me to make sure that the men in question cooperate with any inquiries you make?"

"Yes, your grace."

"If you do not object, I shall turn you back over to Freemantle. He will be immeasurably helpful. And," he eyed Daphne, "I beg that the two of you take dinner with me."

"It will be our pleasure, your grace," she said.

"There is one more thing I should request," Jack said.

Wellington cocked a brow.

"My wife has been ill. I should like a quiet spot for her to rest while I conduct my interviews."

"You shall have it."

* * *

In her mind's eye, Daphne had expected a simple dinner to be taken in the duke's (albeit luxurious) tent. Nothing could have been further from the truth. The officers' mess was a permanent stone building in the village of Lesaca. It featured several wooden tables and chairs, and the cook had prepared a meal comparable to what would be served in any English country home. A lamb had been slaughtered, and the mutton was accompanied by a plentiful assortment of local vegetables and washed down with excellent Spanish wines.

The duke told them each region his armies had traveled to in Spain had its own wine. His personal favorite was Douro wine, which was made from grapes which grew near the River Douro.

"It's my favorite, too," Jack said.

Daphne kept thinking about the duke's poor wife being deprived of her husband's company for months and years at a time. "How long has it been since you've seen Lad---, er, the duchess?" she asked.

The duke's eyes went cold. "It doesn't signify."

What a callous remark! It sounded as if he had little esteem—or love—for his wife.

"Have you never brought her on campaign?" Daphne asked.

"I can think of nothing that would displease me more."

Oh, dear.

Jack was quick to steer conversation away from the obviously unpleasant subject of her grace Wellington. "After seeing the rather luxurious tent you've provided Lady Daphne and I, she will never believe I'm not normally accorded such quarters."

Laughing, the duke eyed Daphne. "I hope you're happy with your accommodation. It was the best I could offer under such hurried circumstances."

"I assure you I could not have been more pleased." She had not expected their tent to be furnished with actual furniture—which it was.

Immediately after dinner, as Jack was continuing with his interviews, Daphne fell asleep and slept all through the night.

When she awakened the following morning, Jack was no more than five feet away from her, snoring rather lustily. He had apparently gone to sleep while writing at the campaign desk in their tent. His cheek was buried in the jumble of papers fanning over the desk's surface, and the pen he must have been clutching had fallen to the ground.

Their second morning together as a married couple and still she was not a proper wife! She sat watching her husband sleep. How happy she was! The former Lady Daphne Chalmers had never thought she would ever have such an admirable husband, would ever travel to Spain. Once more she experienced the same sense of wellbeing she had in the carriage ride to Portsmouth. Just the two of them in an intimate space.

Then she thought of another intimate space—their ship's cabin—and the very idea made her stomach queasy. That was one intimate space she wished she would never see again.

She thoroughly enjoyed watching her husband awaken. He eased himself upright, his spine long, his shoulders powerful. His eyes opened. Immediately upon regaining consciousness, he whirled in her direction.

His dark gaze met hers, and a smile lit up his handsome face. "How are you feeling?" he asked.

She leapt from the bed and came to stand behind him, encircling his upper torso with her arms as her face caressed his. "Wonderful."

All the while, she was trying to read the notes Jack had been making when he fell asleep. "Have you made any progress?"

He ran his hands through his disheveled hair and shook his head.

As she was reading, one name popped out at her as unexpectedly as would her own name inserted into the list of troops: *Major Styles.*

She froze. It had never occurred to her that Cornelia's major would have been at Sorauren! "I know something of Major Styles," she said, almost with reverence as she thought of the man's forlorn widow.

"He died the day after Heffington, so I won't be able to interview him."

Daphne straightened her spine. "Pack up! We're going back to the ship!"

"Have you taken leave of your senses?"

"No, but I'm almost certain the key to our mystery lies in London."

Jack folded his arms across his chest. "I'm not going anywhere until you explain this insanity."

$\mathcal{C}$hapter 6

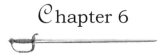

She did not want to tell Jack about her sister's indiscretions. Jack had the moral constitution of a Methodist preacher. She collapsed on the cot. "Someone has got his hands on the major's personal papers. Someone wicked."

"And you know this because?"

"Because my sister Cornelia wrote passionate love letters to Major Styles."

Jack waited a moment for his wife to elaborate, and when she didn't he finally nodded knowingly. "And someone is now blackmailing the duchess."

"I knew my brilliant husband would make the correct deduction."

Jack's eyes narrowed. "Is *brilliant* not one of those words I forbid you to use when speaking of me?"

She was relieved that he was so put out over her praise that he did not lambast her sister's loose morals. "Forgive me, but it *is* just the two of us."

"Tell me everything." His voice was firm.

She related all that Cornelia had told her, and with pride explained how she had been able to eliminate Mrs. Styles from the list of suspects.

Her husband's darkened countenance lifted as she spoke, and when she finished he nodded. "From the interviews I conducted until well past midnight, I had begun to be convinced that Heffington *had* passed the information to the major before he drew his last breath. I've spoken with more than one soldier who saw Styles kneeling beside the dying Heffington."

"I'm not certain that the vile blackmailer has not been apprehended in our absence. I helped Cornelia devise a plan to trap him, but I'm not sure she would carry it out in my absence." She explained the plan to her husband.

His brows were lowered as he was momentarily lost in thought. "Do you think the duchess went through with your plan to put her footmen on the mail coach?"

"I have no way of knowing. While it would be wonderful if she's been able to put a stop to this wretched business in our absence, we must consider other aspects."

"Like the major's batman?"

"Would he not have taken his master's possessions?"

Jack nodded. "I made inquiries along those lines last night. The batman—a fellow by the name of Prufoy—returned to London soon after Sorauren."

"Have you found anyone who might have been in the batman's confidence?"

"No, the man he was closest to died the same day as Major Styles."

"You realize we must return to London at once?"

He peered lovingly at her. "As sorry as I am about your seasickness, having you here with me has proven to be invaluable."

Then he began to gather up his papers.

* * *

They had left Wellington's headquarters fifteen hours after they arrived. Riding like the wind, they reached the awaiting HMS *Avalon* as the sun was setting, and the frigate set sail immediately after they boarded.

She had not thought it possible, but that crossing was considerably worse than the last. As he would empty the chamber pot holding the evidence of her agony and wipe her wet brow with cool clothes, Jack murmured tenderly to her. "I've seen many an experienced sailor succumb to violent retching during storms like this one."

She could well believe the ferocity of the storm, with its high winds and pounding rain, was responsible for her increased anguish.

Even as he spoke the ship pitched at such an angle, Daphne feared they would plunge to the bottom of the sea. In her extreme misery, she almost hoped for it in order to be released from her suffering.

Because of the storm, the return journey took more than twice as long as their initial voyage. Long after the contents of her stomach had been emptied, wicked dry heaves decimated her.

Jack refused to leave her side. Any modesty she had possessed on the earlier crossing vanished. She was too miserable to acknowledge him, but in the foggy recesses of her brain she understood how worried he was. Every nuance of his voice bespoke tenderness. His unflagging attempts to keep her hydrated bespoke his concern. And the touching endearments tumbling from his lips bespoke his love.

His worry did not cease once they reached Portsmouth. He insisted she eat a hearty meal as soon as they landed, even though it was but five in the morning when they took their leave of the accommodating Captain St. James and disembarked the HMS *Avalon*. Jack roused a sleeping innkeeper and explained he would make it worth the man's while if he could put together a meal for them.

He had deposited Daphne in a private parlor there while he procured a traveling coach—again by awakening the proprietor of the establishment.

"It's still dark," the groggy proprietor said. "You sure you have need of a horse at this hour?"

Jack shook his head. "Not a horse. I need to hire a chaise to carry my wife and me to London this morning."

The man was pulling his arm through the sleeve of a coat. "All my coaches is gone."

"Is that not one just inside the inn yard? I was told it belonged to you."

Grabbing his lantern, the man walked to the inn yard with Jack, and with the aid of his lantern light was able to peer at the coach. "I guess me Andy finished puttin' on the new wheel."

"Then it's good to go?"

"If I had a driver."

"Who's Andy?"

"My son."

"Can he drive a coach?"

"As good as anyone, but he's only sixteen. He ain't never been as far away as Lunnon though he has an uncommon interest in studying maps. I daresay he knows as much about Lunnon streets as a Lunnon hackney driver."

A thin youth who was taller than the proprietor poked his head from the door. "Please, Papa, allow me to go to Lunnon. I'm sure I won't get lost on me way."

"I've been the route many times," Jack said. "If you need advice, I shall be at your service."

The lad's father shook his head, a smile dimpling his cheek. "Go wake yer Mam and have her pack you something to eat."

Jack stepped toward the lad. "I will see that you're fed properly, Andy."

The boy flashed a smile at Jack.

"Come along to the inn across the street where my wife and I are eating. You must join us."

"Allow me to fetch me maps."

"He collects them." It was impossible for the father to disguise his pride.

Throughout their breakfast—which Andy ate most heartily—the boy proudly displayed his tall stack of crumpled, grease-stained maps. "This one of Canterbury belonged to a bishop what hired one of me dad's coaches."

It appeared to Jack that Andy had just splotched that town's cathedral with a smudge of runny egg yolk.

"You ever met a Bow Street Runner?" Andy asked Jack.

"Can't say that I have."

"I've seen them," Daphne offered. "You know them by their---"

"Red vests," Andy finished. "A Bow Street Runner must know all the streets in the Capital."

"Your father tells me you know them even though you've never been to London," Jack said.

Andy shrugged his skinny shoulders. "I'm trying to make myself qualified to be a runner."

Daphne favored the lad with a bright smile. "I'm sure you'll be a most diligent one. Tell me, Andy, why do you wish to be a Bow Street Runner?"

"I want to 'elp maidens in distress," he said with a wink. "And I would get great satisfaction from seeing evildoers get their just rewards."

Daphne turned to her husband. "Don't you think Andy will do splendidly?"

"Indeed I do."

* * *

Many hours later, the glistening dome of London's St. Paul's came into view. "I believe we should go first to Lankersham House," Jack said as they crossed Westminster Bridge.

It was remarkable how parallel their thoughts were. She had been thinking the same thing. Had Daphne's plan to install the duke's footmen on the Penzance coach been successful, it was possible the blackmailer—who must also be in possession of Captain Heffington's list—had already been unmasked.

Going strictly on her own intuition, though, Daphne did not think that plan had succeeded. She could not be sure it had even been carried out in her absence. Cornelia was the most indolent woman imaginable. Without her elder sister prodding, she tended to put things off for vast stretches of time, seemingly thinking that if unpleasant situations were out of her mind, they would resolve themselves.

Daphne was reminded of the time Cornelia had hidden one of her lovers beneath her high tester bed when the duke had returned unexpectedly early from his shooting lodge in Scotland. With Cornelia incapable of addressing the problem of how to remove one (very hungry) lover for two full days, the exasperated man finally waited until duchess and duke were soundly asleep above him, then he stealthily stole away in the night—only to be apprehended by an overzealous footman.

Fortunately, the lover was able to bribe the footman, and everything—except Cornelia's little *flirtation*—ended well.

As Daphne and Jack went to depart the coach in front of the huge iron gates of Lankersham House, Daphne saw Virginia leave the baroque mansion. "Uh, oh. I cannot see Virginia just now. Have the coachman circle the square once more."

Jack did as she instructed. "Why do you not want to see the duchess's twin?"

"Because she does not know about the blackmail, and Cornelia forbid me to tell her."

"I thought you said the twins shared everything."

"Not everything. Virginia disapproves of Cornelia's . . . *flirtations*, as Cornelia calls them."

"How refreshing. An aristocrat who takes her marriage vows seriously."

"You would adore Virginia were you around her more. She is not only completely besotted over her Sir Ronald, she is the sweetest person in the three kingdoms. She's a natural nurturer."

"Like you."

She shook her head. "No, I'm afraid I'm just the domineering firstborn."

The coach once more came to a stop in front of Lankersham House. As they went to step down, Jack turned to her. "I know you are a most discreet female, but I want to caution you. You are not to mention the duchess's indiscretions. To anyone. Ever."

"Of course, I wouldn't."

"Will she be upset you've told me about the letters?"

"Under normal circumstances, she would. But she seems to believe you some spy extraordinaire who is the only person in the kingdom who can extricate her from this predicament." Daphne held up her hands. "I swear I did not tell her you were a spy extraordinaire! *Extraordinaire* is too suspiciously close to one of those words you barred me from using—when I speak of you."

He gazed at her from narrowed eyes.

When he faced the Duchess of Lankersham a moment later, he was all smiles. Though she was not seeing callers this day, she welcomed the Drydens into her private sitting room. Daphne could not understand why one would have subjected herself to the rigors of having her hair dressed, squeezing her bosom into stays, and dressing in such lovely gowns if one was not seeing callers. In her golden dress—which revealed too much of her breasts for Daphne's taste—the duchess was uncommonly beautiful. No wonder she had been able to snare a duke.

"You are back!" a delighted Cornelia said. "I declare, that is the fastest trip to the Peninsula I've ever heard of." Her brows lowered. "Have you seen Mama? She's been beside herself with worry over you."

"No," Daphne said. "We came to you first. Were you able to install your footmen on the Penzance mail coach?"

Cornelia settled herself on a settee of scarlet silk, folding her hands in her lap. "You will be happy to know, I did. I wished to show you I am not indolent."

"Then you were able to discover the identity of your blackmailer?"

Cornelia's face fell, her huge chocolate eyes regarding Jack. "He knows?"

"Of course," Daphne responded. "You told me you thought he was the only one in the kingdom who could help you."

"He knows everything?"

Daphne frowned. "Everything."

The duchess's long lashes lowered, then she brightened. "Well, I got two very strong—and I must add, very handsome—footmen and concocted some story to put Lankersham off. My maid saw that the footmen, who were, of course, dressed in postal livery, made it onto the coach, and she personally put my bag of money with the other bags. The Lankersham footmen were to observe it at all times, and when someone tried to take it, they were instructed to apprehend the rascal."

Jack frowned. "From your expression, I take it the plan failed."

Cornelia nodded. "By the time the coach reached Camberley the money had completely disappeared. The footmen admitted to a lapse, and apparently that was all it took."

"Had passengers departed the coach that soon?" Jack asked.

"Yes, I thought to ask that," Cornelia said. "One. A French lady."

"That French lady must have been the one," Daphne said.

"D'Arblier may have a hand in this," Jack muttered.

"Dearest, you obsess too much about that blasted duc."

Jack's mouth folded into a grim line.

* * *

Striding toward the waiting carriage, Jack asked Daphne if she wished to go to Sidworth House. She stopped in mid stride, tilted her face to his—which was just inches away—and glared. "I have been married six days now and have yet to cross the threshold of our home with you by my side." While Jack had been whiling away his time in Brighton, Daphne had placed their wedding gifts there and had hung in Jack's bedchamber— or, directed the hanging of—the wedding portrait she'd painted of Warrior.

"You know I must go to the War Office to learn the direction of Styles' batman?" Jack said.

"Of course."

"I'll just dismiss the carriage, and go around the corner to fetch Warrior."

"Since we're going to be making inquiries together, I thought perhaps we could keep the carriage another day or so. It shouldn't cost that much more. . . What do you think?" She had decided that, contrary what Cornelia expected, she was not going to be a domineering wife. Jack wouldn't like it at all if she started ordering him about.

His dark eyes flashed with mirth. "Very well, my lady. Keeping the coach does seem to make sense."

As their coach came to their narrow, three-storey house, he asked, "Should you like me to carry you over the threshold?"

"Not at all. You must get to Whitehall while there is still someone there who can assist you! It will be dark soon." She kissed him on the cheek as she exited the carriage.

While Jack was telling Andy they would require the carriage one more day, Daphne noticed the lad's boots had a hole in the sole. "It has occurred to me that your mother may be worried about you if you don't return by tomorrow," she said to the lad. "Should you like me to dispatch a letter to her, informing her we shall need your services a bit longer?"

"I should be ever so grateful." He gave Daphne his mother's name and direction.

Beholding their modest house filled Daphne with pride. The brick house had been painted white long before Daphne had been born. Despite its small size, she thought the house's white paint rather set it apart from its nearby neighbors. And though she did not possess the keen eye for such things as her sisters possessed, she thought their home exuded good taste.

She immediately dubbed it Dryden House. It had belonged to her great grandmother in the years of her widowhood. If Daphne and Jack had a daughter, it would one day go to her.

The very notion of having a daughter, having Jack's child, caused something vibrant to unfurl within her. She felt as if she had drunk an entire bottle of champagne as she strolled across the pavement to ascend the steps to the shiny black door and let herself into the house. There was but a single servant, owing to the uncertainty over the Drydens' return.

Without being aware of what she was doing, she climbed the stairs to the top floor where the bedchambers were located, and she came to stand before Jack's big bed. With Cornelia's help, Daphne had selected a manly red for the velvet curtains which surrounded the bed and which draped the chamber's two tall windows.

She ran her hand over the scarlet velvet covering the bed, the bed where she would finally sleep beside her husband. In just a few hours, she would belong to him in every way. Her heartbeat drummed, and her breath grew short.

She knew she must leave the room. Taking a quick look at Warrior's portrait which hung over the chimneypiece, she went to the next room: her bedchamber. Their lone chambermaid had hung most of her clothing or folded it into the linen press.

Since it was much cooler in London than it had been in Spain, she decided to fetch a velvet pelisse. She wanted to be ready to join Jack as soon as he returned. The sooner they got to the batman, the better.

* * *

Jack was actually pleased that his wife had suggested they keep the carriage another day. He didn't want her traipsing around London at night on a horse, which he knew she would have insisted upon. It was too damned cold. She needed the shelter the carriage would provide.

He was entirely too worried about her, though he had tried to keep his worries to himself. The two wretched sea voyages had racked her body so ruthlessly, she had lost a great deal of weight—something she could ill afford to do.

Secretary of War Lord Palmerston had been enormously helpful at the War Office. In mere minutes the efficient man had located the address for Major Styles' batman, Eli Prufoy. "I believe that's not very far from here," Palmerston had said, "just off the Strand."

"Thank you, my lord. You've been most helpful." As Jack left the building he thought of the letter of introduction Lord Castlereagh had provided for him. Between Lord Castlereagh and the Prince Regent, Jack was assured of being treated as if he were a royal duke.

* * *

The moment the carriage drew up in front of the house, his exuberant wife threw open the front door and came racing toward the carriage.

First, she addressed the coachman. "You will be pleased to know I sent off the letter to your mother and was told it would reach her in the morning."

Andy thanked her as he assisted her into the carriage.

By now, night had fallen, and the streets were filled with conveyances clopping along the Strand, snarling the pace. He would have made far better progress were he on horseback, but he knew Daphne wanted to be active in these inquiries.

"What is the name of the street?" she asked as she squinted out the window as lanterns were being lit outside the shops they passed.

"How do you know I got the batman's address?"

"Because I just know."

"Cotton Lane. Lord Palmerston said it's just off the Strand."

"How in the world would Cupid know that?"

"Cupid?"

"That's what Lady Cowper calls Lord Palmerston. He's her lover, you know."

Jack just rolled his eyes. But secretly he was proud of the woman he had married. She knew everyone in the *ton* and was uncommonly popular.

Soon the coach came to a stop at the entrance to a lane not wide enough for the carriage to pass. "I believe we've reached Cotton Lane. Should you like to join me, my lady?" One glance at the dark, narrow lane, though, and he was sorry that he had brought Daphne. A cutthroat could be right around the corner, and they'd never see him. Foolishly, Jack had come off without a weapon—something he vowed *not* to do again. At least, not at night when Daphne was with him. After they walked along eighty yards or so, the lane terminated at a large courtyard ringed with narrow wooden houses. These crooked, ancient houses threatened to topple into the courtyard.

"What number did you say?" she asked.

"Twelve."

"It's so dark, I can't read the numbers."

"If someone should enter this god-forsaken place, we could ask."

No sooner had the words left his mouth than two boys came running into the square. "Pardon me," Jack said to them, "could you tell me which one is Number 12?"

They halted. "Yer standing in front of it," the taller of the two said.

Jack and Daphne both turned to stare at the quiet house which was completely dark. "We're trying to find the gentleman who lives here. A Mr. Prufoy," Daphne explained.

"You won't find 'im here no more." Again, it was the taller of the two who spoke.

"Then he's moved?" Jack asked.

"No. He died."

$\mathcal{C}$hapter 7

"Oh, dear," Daphne said.

"It was in the *Morning Chronicle.*" Had the lad been racing through his memorization of Hamlet's soliloquy, he could not have spoken with more pride.

"The announcement of his death?" Jack asked.

The boys looked at one another, and they shrugged in unison. "More like the story of a tavern brawl," the taller one said.

Daphne's mouth gaped open. "He was killed in a tavern brawl?"

Both lads nodded. "Just around the corner at the Cock & Stalk public house."

"Then no one else lived here? Had the man no family?" Daphne asked.

"None what I know of."

Jack took coins from his pocket and gave one to each of the lads. "Thank you. You've been most helpful."

"Thank *you*, guvnah!"

How in the bloody hell did a soldier get through all those battles in the Peninsula only to come home and die in a tavern brawl just steps from his home? As he and Daphne went back over the same cobbled lane they had arrived on, Jack cautioned his wife. "This is not a good place for a lady after dark. You're to stay inside the carriage while I make inquiries at the public house."

His exasperating wife stiffened, and her voice turned brittle. "I most certainly will not stay safe in the carriage while you interview those at the tavern! As highly intelligent as you are—and do not argue with me about that—you are a man, and men don't always think of the right questions to ask. They lack the proper curiosity for thorough inquiries."

"Ladies are not supposed to be in public houses."

She practically snorted. "As if someone would dare to question it when I enter with an officer of the Regent's own hussars!"

She was likely right. And he did possess the letter of introduction from Lord Castlereagh which was better than guineas in hand. He sighed. "I *will* feel better if I have you with me."

"You're afraid of those men in the tavern?"

"Certainly not! What I meant is that I will worry less about *you* if you are with me."

She squeezed his hand. "I do appreciate your concern for my wellbeing, dearest. I haven't properly thanked you for your wonderful care of me when we were on the ship."

He was relieved that light from some new gas lamps on the Strand spilled into Cotton Lane now. Soon after turning onto the Strand, he saw the sign for the Cock & Stalk swinging from chains. It featured a bright red rooster sitting on pile of celery stalks. Still holding hands, with Daphne lifting her skirts to avoid contact with errant plops of horse dung, they crossed the busy street.

"You're to stay at my side. Understood?"

She executed a mock salute. "Yes, captain."

It was still too early for public houses to have drawn much of a crowd. The disadvantage to that was the inability to interview eyewitnesses; the advantage, they would have better access to the establishment's proprietor.

When he and Daphne entered, several men turned to gawk at Daphne. As much as he loved his wife, Jack knew she was no beauty. Her gender and the fact she was obviously Quality had roused the men's interest. With her fingers digging into his forearm, the pair of them strolled to the long bar. While more than twenty men could easily have lined the long, wooden structure, no more than eight did so at this early hour. Twice that number, with bumpers in hand, stood in clusters around the dimly lit room, which had hushed as soon as Daphne walked in.

A shaggy-haired, redheaded man of middle age addressed them from the other side of the long bar. "What can I get for ye?" His eye roved to Daphne.

"I wish to know about the last minutes of Eli Prufoy," Jack said.

"Ah! Ye must 'av served in the army with the gent!"

"Indeed, I did."

"It's sorry I am that one of our brave soldiers met his end at the Cock & Stalk." The redhead shook his head ruefully. "You can read all about it in the *Morning Chronicle*. I've got the newspaper account right 'ere." He whipped out a yellowing, much-read newspaper and handed it to Jack. "Ye and the missus can read it over by the lamp." He indicated an oil lamp behind the bar.

They took the newspaper to the end of the bar and stepped just behind its curved end to get closer to the lamp, which was stowed out of reach from possible overly active patrons. The story of Eli Prufoy's death was on the front page. A pity a man had to die to be accorded such notice.

Returning Soldier
Meets His End in
Tavern Brawl Just
Steps from His Home

An occurrence most vile took place on the night of April 11 when one Eli Prufoy, of the Life Guards. who just recently returned from many years of service in Spain, lost his life as the result of brawl in a public house near his home.

Angus MacKenzie, the proprietor of the Cock & Stalk located on London's Strand, said Mr. Prufoy had been a regular patron of his establishment since he returned from Spain last month, and the former soldier had never caused any problems before.

"He was always pleasant and a bit quiet," Mr. MacKenzie said. "I was surprised to find him wrestling with a pair of men right out of the blue."

The public house's proprietor said he'd never before seen the two men who fought with Mr. Prufoy. They left the valiant soldier dying on the floor of the Cock & Stalk.

Mr. MacKenzie expressed shock when he found Mr. Prufoy unresponsive. "I have seen my share of brawls before, but the men have always been able to walk away."

A surgeon, Mr. Billingsley, was called. He was attempting to administer aid during Mr. Prufoy's final minutes.

As soon as Jack finished reading the account, he knew that it had been no tavern brawl.

It had been murder.

Daphne strolled behind the bar to the proprietor. "Mr. MacKenzie?"

He handed a bumper of ale to a scruffy patron in well-soiled clothing. "Aye, me lady?"

Jack had come to stand behind his bride. How in the hell did the redheaded man know Daphne was a lady?

"Can you describe the two men who fought with Mr. Prufoy?" she asked sweetly.

MacKenzie shrugged. "Everything 'appened so fast. And me establishment was excessively crowded that night—which meant I was excessively busy. When I heard the commotion, I turned to look, to try to recognize which of me patrons were involved. I mostly only saw Prufoy. Didn't take much notice of the other men."

"Hair color? Clothing? Were they dressed as Quality, for example?" she asked.

MacKenzie shook his head. "No, not Quality like yerselves. They wore dark clothes, and their hair was dark, sort of. Leastways, it was brown."

"Age?" Daphne asked.

He shrugged again. "Average age. Maybe thirty. Average height. Everything about them was average."

Including their brown hair, Jack thought. Exactly as he would have expected. "Did you perchance hear them speak?" Jack particularly wondered if they might have spoken with a French accent.

"I don't remember 'earing 'em speak."

Jack stepped forward. "Can you direct us to the surgeon?"

"He's right here on the Strand. Ye can find him above the dentist down on the right."

Jack gave the man a shilling. "Thank you."

As they went to walk away, MacKenzie said, "Captain?"

Jack spun around to face him.

"I want you to know the Cock 'n Stalk's a safe place."

"I believe you."

* * *

The surgeon's rather large family lived in the cramped quarters above the dentist's shop, which was still open even though it was nine o'clock at night. Daphne's heart went out to these people who had to toil twelve and more hours a day, six days a week.

In almost total darkness, she and Jack climbed up the steep and narrow wooden stairway and rapped at the only door on the landing. A young woman who could not have been much older than Daphne, but who had one babe hitched to her side and a toddler clutching at her skirts, opened the door.

"Is Mr. Billingsley in?" Jack asked.

She shook her head.

"Is this where we can locate the surgeon, Mr. Billingsley?" Daphne inquired.

Upon hearing their cultured voices, the woman smoothed back the loose tendrils of golden hair that had fallen about her face and offered them a smile. "Indeed it is. I'm Mrs. Billingsley." Her voice was genteel but lacked the casual languidness that characterized the aristocracy. The woman reminded Daphne of her governess, Miss Queensbury, which reminded Daphne that when she was nine or ten she had thought a woman of four and twenty frightfully ancient.

"Do you know where we can reach your husband?" Daphne asked.

Mrs. Billingsley's blue eyes danced. "That is a very good question. I've been keeping his dinner warm these three hours past."

"I daresay a surgeon's life is a busy one," Jack said. "Would it be agreeable if we checked back in, say, an hour?"

"You're welcome to wait in here. It's not very tidy, what with five little ones running around, but you're more than welcome to come in."

Before Jack could refuse, Daphne accepted. "That is very kind of you."

Their hostess swung open her door.

"Allow me to introduce myself. I'm Lady Daphne, and this is my husband, Captain Dryden." How natural it sounded to call Jack her husband! How vastly exciting! Even though they had been married for six days, she had not had the opportunity to introduce herself as Jack's wife before. She would have to find more opportunities of doing so.

As she sauntered into the Billingsley family rooms, careful not to step on toy soldiers and rag dolls that littered the otherwise clean wooden floors, Daphne was enumerating incidents in which she could practice saying she was Jack's wife. She would interview for a new housekeeper. *May I introduce my husband, Captain Dryden. . .*

They walked past a wooden table where a lad of eight or nine sat, furiously writing. She slowed down to peer at what he wrote, and saw that he had filled a page with mathematical problems. "A most industrious lad."

"I fear my husband's too severe upon him."

Daphne turned to regard the woman. "He must be the firstborn."

"Indeed he is."

"I, too, am a firstborn," Daphne said, shrugging, "and I was a great deal more studious than the siblings who came after me. Each child was less studious than the one in front of her. 'Tis a wonder the youngest isn't a complete moron."

Mrs. Billingsley and Jack laughed.

Mrs. Billingsley set her babe on a woolen rug while she went to remove a stack of folded laundry from the sofa so Jack and Daphne could sit there.

The outer door swung open, and a tall, gaunt man with a black leather medical bag strode into the room.

"It's my husband," Mrs. Billingsley said. She was unable to conceal her pride.

The man, who appeared to be a decade older than his wife, flicked his gaze to the visitors.

Jack stood. "Allow me to introduce myself. I'm Captain Jack Dryden, and this is my wife, Lady Daphne." The two men shook hands.

Though Daphne most certainly liked to hear Jack introduce her as his wife, she regretted that she'd not had the opportunity to once more introduce Jack as *my husband*.

"How can I be of service to you?" The surgeon asked Jack.

"I wished to inquire about the death of Eli Prufoy."

The man nodded. "Ah, yes. At the Cock & Stalk." He ran his eye over Jack's regimentals. "You must have served with the man. I understand he'd been under Lord Wellesley's command."

Daphne practically bit her tongue to prevent herself from informing him that Lord Wellesley was now the Duke of Wellington—a man she had actually met! She still could scarcely believe she had taken dinner with the field marshal, that she had actually been to Spain! She could almost forget the wretched sea voyage that had taken her there.

Almost.

"Yes," Jack said.

"Won't you sit down?" the surgeon asked. Mrs. Billingsley by then had removed the clean laundry from the sofa before scooping up the baby, who'd started crying.

"I'll be putting the children to bed now," she said.

Daphne thanked the woman for her hospitality. She was relieved that the children were being taken away. Children, in Daphne's opinion, did not need to hear about dying men and tavern brawls.

"Can you explain to me what kind of wounds Mr. Prufoy suffered?" Jack asked.

"Lacerations. All over the poor man's body."

Jack's brows lowered. "Is this, do you think, consistent with injuries from fisticuffs—most particularly from men in their cups?"

The surgeon pursed his lips. "I had no reason to think otherwise. There were a number of eyewitnesses present who had observed the fight."

"Was the tavern well lit?"

If, on April 11, it looked as it had earlier that evening, Daphne thought, it had to have been quite dark.

"No, it wasn't," the surgeon said.

"Do you think it's possible Mr. Prufoy could have been killed with a knife?" Jack inquired.

"It certainly is. Actually, that was my assumption when I initially viewed the man's injuries. He appeared to have suffered puncture wounds to the abdomen and chest. There was a great deal of blood loss. But when I queried the observers, no one claims to have seen a knife."

"Which could be explained, given the lack of light in the establishment," Daphne said.

"Indeed."

"Had the man or men who had fought with Prufoy left the premises by the time of your arrival?"

"That's what those who were present said. I believe Mr. Prufoy had been overmanned by a pair of men, and it's my understanding these man had not previously been to the Cock & Stalk."

Oh, dear. That must mean poor Eli Prufoy had been murdered—which, apparently, her husband had apparently already deduced.

Jack stood. "I'm indebted to you for answering my questions."

Daphne remained seated. She was not about to leave yet, not when there was more to be learned. "I believe the proprietor of the Cock & Stalk told us you were with the unfortunate Mr. Prufoy when he drew his last breath."

"That is correct."

"Did he try to speak?" she asked.

The surgeon nodded.

Jack looked skeptical. "But surely you couldn't hear him."

"You could have heard a pin drop in the room that night as dozens of sobering men gathered around the wretched man lying in a pool of his own blood."

Daphne's pulse galloped. "Can you tell us what he said?"

"He called for his wife."

"I don't believe he was married," Daphne said.

Jack nodded. "According to the neighbors, he lived alone, and the war office has no record of any payments being made to any Mrs. Prufoy. I checked there just today."

"Then it must have been his ladybird." Mr. Billingsley tossed an apologetic glance at Daphne. "Forgive me, my lady, for discussing such matters."

"Think nothing of it. I *am* a married woman." She rather enjoyed saying that, even if she had yet to truly understand exactly what occurred in a marriage bed. Her heartbeat accelerated. By tomorrow morning she would have learned all there was to know about that particularly intriguing subject.

She leaned closer. "Did he call her by name?"

"Yes. Her name was Fanny."

Daphne personally knew at least two dozen ladies named Fanny. "Did he, perchance, use a last name as well?"

The surgeon pursed his lips as he nodded. "I believe he did. I thought he was asking for ale. He would say *Fanny. Ale.* Finally, I realized her name must be Fanny Hale, and in his dying breath he confirmed it."

Daphne's glittering eyes met Jack's. "Oh, Mr. Billingsley, you have been extraordinarily helpful!"

They took their leave of the surgeon, and as they were walking down the dark stairway to the pavement below, she said, "Why did you not tell me you knew Mr. Prufoy had been murdered?"

"I didn't *know* it."

"But we do now."

"It does seem so."

This particular stretch of the Strand had come alive at night. Most of the shop windows were still lighted, and a steady stream of men was funneling into the Cock & Stalk.

"Dearest?" She casually peered through a window into the linen draper's where a few matrons were casting about selecting what looked to be sensible woolens.

"Yes?"

"Where in London would a lonely soldier go to find a woman to . . ."

"You're not going there."

"But we must. The very future of England could depend upon it."

She eyed a queue of men winding from a shop and wondered what was being sold there that could attract so many customers. She and Jack snaked around the line, and she cast a glance at the shop window. A print shop. She paused to gape at the print which was prominently displayed in the window. Then she quickly looked away from the lewd print, her cheeks hot. "A shocking waste of pence, it seems to me."

When they arrived at their awaiting carriage near the entrance to Cotton Lane, Jack grudgingly told Andy to take them to Covent Garden.

$\mathcal{C}$hapter 8

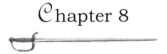

It wasn't as if she had not been to the Covent Garden area at night before. The theatre and the opera were located near the huge flower market. She had not, though, actually walked the pavement there at night. Lord and Lady Sidworth made certain their daughters were immediately whisked into an awaiting carriage as soon as they left the theatre.

Now that she was strolling along with Jack, who was doing his best to ignore the dozens of pleas to purchase nosegays, she was seeing for the first time things she had never before seen. That these flower sellers were decked out in dress upon tattered dress indicated to Daphne that they wore everything they possessed, likely because they had no permanent home.

She noticed, too, the proliferation of bagnios along both sides of the street and was able to observe uncommonly indecent-looking women lasciviously entering these questionable establishments rather too intimately on the arms of men they had likely just met.

Jack was not in a good humor. "I don't like your being here," he grumbled.

"I will remind you that I *am* a married woman." Which she would rather enjoy shouting from the spire of Westminster Abbey.

"You are a complete innocent."

She paused right there on the pavement beneath the moonlit sky, looked up into his smoldering black eyes, and lowered her voice to a husky purr. "I won't be by tomorrow morning."

Jack drew a deep breath and pushed forward without responding. Even though he would not articulate it, she knew he desired her.

They were coming abreast of a woman who looked perfectly the sort who would give physical comfort to a lonely soldier. As they came closer, Daphne realized the dark-haired female was not a woman, after all. She could not be more than eighteen. If she was that old. The rosy cheeked girl stood at the apex where Chandos and another street Daphne could not name came together. The bodice of her scarlet dress barely contained the two large spheres of her breasts.

Daphne strode up to the girl, despite that Jack was attempting to tug his wife in the opposite direction. "Pardon me, but I was wondering if you know a lady by the name of Fanny Hale." Daphne could see beneath the lantern light that a thick coat of rouge covered the girl's smooth cheeks. From this close an examination, it was also evident this girl was far younger than eighteen.

Her pale blue eyes swept over Daphne from the top of her velvet pelisse to the tips of her expensive satin slippers. "What's it worth?"

Daphne's quizzing gaze darted to Jack.

"Five pence," he said.

"Let me see yer money."

Jack produced the coins.

The girl snatched them up, dropped them into the snug bodice of her faded brown dress, then met Daphne's gaze. "So ye asks me if I knows a woman what goes by the name of Fanny 'ale? Well, me answer is *no*!" She spun away and raced toward the Strand as if her skirts were on fire.

Jack smirked. "A most enterprising girl."

"Quite true. My consolation must be that she has need of the money."

"May I suggest you allow me to handle the next query?"

"You may suggest anything you like, but me answer is *no*."

Their gazes locked, and they both broke out laughing.

"I know how to interrogate, madam. I was merely being a polite gentleman with the lady to whom I am wed."

"I adore the sound of that: *to whom I am wed*. It will be such great fun being married to you." She linked her arm through his. "You see, if I weren't married to you, I wouldn't be able to be here right now."

"Enlighten me, please, on why it is a good thing Lady Daphne Dryden is here right now strolling alongside the Covent Garden prostitutes."

"Daphne Dryden! I never thought of myself quite like that before. It's so wonderfully alliterative, is it not?"

"It is, but I shouldn't like our children saddled with names like Dorcus Dryden. Sounds much too forced."

Our children. She could positively melt into the pavement at the thought. She squeezed her husband's hand but, wishing for his words to linger in the air, said nothing.

"Since Eli Prufoy was in his forties, I thought perhaps his Fannie Hale might not be a young woman, might perhaps be a woman he's known for years."

Daphne looked puzzled. "Then you don't think she'll be in this area?"

"I did not say that. Take a look around. The women here span all ages."

She nodded thoughtfully. It occurred to her that most of the pedestrians they passed were men. She found herself wondering if Jack had ever come there looking for a woman with whom to slake his manly hunger. As curious a being as she normally was and as much as she wanted to know *most* everything about Jack's life before he met her, that particular kind of intimacy was a matter she did not want to know about.

Was she afraid to learn he might have been in love before? If he had, the lady would have been a beauty, and Daphne positively did not want to know anything about it. Better to delude herself that their lives began on the day they met.

He gritted his teeth. "This would be easier were you not with me."

"Initially, yes, I can see where it would be. But what if you find Fanny Hale? I must be present during your *interrogation*, as you call it. I can think of things to ask that you do not. Remember, at Mr. Billingsley's you were ready to leave after asking questions about the wounds. It was I who thought to ask about dying words."

"I will give you that. Finding the woman who was in Prufoy's confidence is our strongest hope of learning what happened to Heffington's list."

"If there was a list."

They both grew solemn.

Over the next half hour, Jack politely asked several of the older women of the night if they knew Fanny Hale. None of the women either knew a woman by that name, nor did they have a suggestion for another place Jack and Daphne might look.

Despite their discouraging lack of progress, Daphne brightened. "If we don't find the woman tonight we can put an advertisement in the newspapers asking for her to come forward."

"Finding her tonight has rather the same odds as running into the Regent's daughter walking the streets in Covent Garden." He paused. "The newspaper suggestion would be a good one, save for two drawbacks."

She looked up at him. "What drawbacks?"

"First, not many women who ply their wares in this neighborhood read newspapers. I daresay most of them cannot even read. And . . . if they could read and did have the opportunity to get their hands on a seven pence newspaper—which is highly unlikely—more precious time will lapse."

She knew the wisdom of her husband's words. Even more sobering was the sudden realization that she might have been completely wrong in thinking Fanny Hale was a prostitute. "Has it occurred to you that our Fanny may be a perfectly respectable woman?"

"Regrettably."

But he continued to question perfectly unrespectable women in a most respectful manner.

Long after the theatres had emptied of their finely dressed patrons and after midnight had passed, he finally got a lead.

On a much quieter street a few blocks north of Covent Garden Jack approached a woman carrying a basket of fresh vegetables. Despite having looked at demireps all night, Daphne still did not possess a discerning enough eye to determine if a woman was . . . or wasn't. This one dressed more respectably because she wore only one dress—of sensible dark bombazine—and its neckline was not terribly low. She must actually have a residence and must be heading there now.

Jack stepped slightly into the woman's path. "I beg your pardon, madam. I am looking for a woman named Fanny Hale, and I was wondering if you might be acquainted with her."

The woman, who looked to be nearing forty, flicked her gaze to Daphne, then back to Jack. Daphne found herself wondering if this woman was going home to a husband or to children. "That I am. She's me neighbor."

"I would be much obliged," Jack said, "if you could direct us to her."

She nodded solemnly. "Poor dear, she 'asn't been the same since---"

"Since her soldier was killed," Jack finished.

The lady's eyes rounded, then trailed along Jack's regimental jacket. "You must 'ave served with Prufoy."

Jack inclined his head. "We both served in the Peninsula for many years."

Daphne noticed how her husband had answered the woman's question without telling a direct falsehood. He hated it when the code of honor and honesty which guided his life had to be compromised sometimes in the course of his clandestine duties.

"Mrs. 'ale, lives right across the hall from me."

Daphne stepped up to stand beside Jack. "My husband and I will be ever so grateful to you for directing us to Mrs. Hale." Daphne believed that the fact they were a husband and wife gave them a certain credibility, even trustworthiness.

"I can do better 'n that. Ye can follow me 'ome."

"How very kind of you," Jack said. "Here, allow me to carry your basket."

"I must caution you," she said as she handed the basket to Jack and lowered her voice, "that the lady what owns our building don't tolerate noisemaking on the stairs none late at night."

"We will be as quiet as mice," Daphne promised.

"Allow me to introduce myself," Jack said. "I am Captain Jack Dryden, and this is my wife, Lady Daphne."

The woman's head whirled to peer at Daphne. "A real lady?"

"Indeed," Jack answered.

"Won't Fanny be bowled over? I wish our landlady was awake so I could introduce her to our friend, Lady Daphne." As she spoke, she started up the steps to a tall, narrow brick building. "Me name's Bess. I goes by Mrs. Johnson."

Though Daphne's knowledge of the demimonde was minute, she did know that women who subsisted by selling their bodies typically adopted the name *Mrs.* even though many of them had never married. She suspected that practice might have been started to give an unmarried mother a sense of respectability.

"It's a pleasure to meet you, Mrs. Johnson," Jack said. He and Daphne followed her up the steps into the dark building. They quietly began to climb the unlit stairs. Mrs. Johnson came to a stop on the top floor, held her index finger to her lips, and whispered, "This be my room." She glanced across the dark hall. "Fanny be there."

Jack gave her a shilling. "We are most indebted to you, madam."

"Oh, thank you, Captain!" In her excitement, she had inadvertently raised her voice.

Daphne had already begun to rap softly at Fanny's door. When a minute had passed and still there was no response, she shrugged, then began to rap more loudly.

Another minute passed, and Daphne's knock sharpened. This time it resulted in stirring behind the closed door.

The door opened slightly, and a woman's face appeared in the narrow opening. "Yes?"

"Hello," Daphne said brightly. "I am Lady Daphne Dryden, and my husband and I seek Mrs. Fanny Hale."

"That'd be me."

"We're frightfully sorry for disturbing you at such a late hour," Daphne said, "but we wished to speak to you about Eli Prufoy."

The sleepy woman did not say anything for a moment. Then she uttered, "I'm not dressed properly."

"Oh," Daphne said, "we don't mind waiting while you slip into your clothing. We can stay right here in the corridor."

A few minutes later, a candle in hand, Mrs. Hale opened the door and asked them to come in. Even after Daphne and Jack followed her into the chambers, she kept her voice low.

The rust-colored head of a sleeping boy lying on a pallet just inside the adjacent room indicated to Daphne that children were sleeping there. "Please be seated, my lady." Mrs. Hale indicated a sofa.

Then her eyes met Jack's. "Ye must 'ave served with me Mr. Prufoy."

"Indeed I did."

"He was as fine a man as ever lived," said Mrs. Hale as she dabbed at her face with the sleeve of her woolen gown. "I don't believe he would ever have started no tavern brawl. He was the most kind and gentle man." She shook her head. "And he was sick of fighting and killin'."

Daphne judged the woman to be in her late twenties or possibly early thirties. There was a wholesomeness about her lightly freckled appearance that made it difficult to believe this woman with warm brown hair could ever have been a prostitute. Perhaps it was her modest woolen dress that leant her respectability, or perhaps it was the children sleeping in the next room. It could even have been the way she had a propensity to smile shyly, even though everything in her countenance demonstrated her grief. She had about her the look of a rounded favored aunt.

"We have strong reason to believe Mr. Prufoy was followed to the Cock & Stalk public house by men who intended to kill him," Jack said.

Mrs. Hale's mouth gaped open, and her eyes filled with tears. "Who would ever want a kindly man like him to be dead?"

Jack shrugged. "We think perhaps he was killed for some papers that might have been in his possession."

She nodded. "I remember him telling me he had important papers to take to an important man."

"Did he perchance mention Lord Castlereagh?" Jack asked.

She shook her head. "To tell ye the truth, I don't remember the man's name. I might know it if I 'eard it, and I do remember it being a lord. I'd have remembered if it was Lord Castlereagh, though, because I know he's the Foreign Secretary."

"Did Mr. Prufoy tell you what was in the papers?" Jack asked.

"Not really. He said his Major—you know my Eli was batman to Major Styles—was killed in battle, and that before he died, he told Eli to deliver the important papers to some Lord Something."

Daphne's heartbeat stampeded. There had been a list! And it had made it back to England!

But now it had fallen into the wrong hands, and it was imperative they get it back.

"Did your Mr. Prufoy ever mention being in possession of love letters written to Major Styles from a woman other than his wife?"

She nodded. "He returned the rest of the major's things to his widow but me Eli didn't 'av the 'eart to let her see those letters. Me Eli could be very discreet. He told me the love letters were written by some mighty duchess, but Eli was too much the gentleman to name 'er even to me."

"Then I doubt a gentleman like that would ever consider trying to blackmail that *mighty* duchess?" Daphne mumbled.

"Ye can be assured that Eli wouldn't do nothing illegal like that! Why, he was such a fine man, he wouldn't even move in with me here when I begged 'im to. Said it wouldn't be proper fer me children to see that." She looked up at Daphne, her eyes misting. "I know what ye must be thinking. Why didn't he marry me? Well, the truth is, I ain't at liberty to marry because me 'usband, who abandoned me and the young ones, is still alive though I 'aven't seen 'im in more than six years."

The poor woman. "I'm so terribly sorry over your loss," Daphne said. "Mr. Prufoy must have been a wonderful man."

"Aye, he was that."

"And I'm sorry that we had to disturb you so late in the night," Jack added, "but it's very important. If you should ever remember the lord's name, please come to us. I will write down our direction." His gaze flicked to Daphne.

"Oh, dearest, I have the cards I had printed with our new address." She reached into her reticule, extracted one from her mother-of-pearl case, and handed it to Mrs. Hale as she also tucked a guinea into the woman's hand.

* * *

They trudged six blocks from Mrs. Hale's to their waiting carriage. She did not want to admit to Jack how weary she was as she nearly collapsed into the carriage. Ever since she had been so dreadfully ill on the ship—good lord, could that have been this same day?—he'd been prodigiously worried about her.

It had certainly been an eventful day since they'd departed the HMS *Avalon* early that morning nearly four and twenty hours ago. No wonder she was so fatigued.

The streets were not so crowded at this time of morning. Their carriage whisked over to Dryden House in just a few minutes.

"I must show you your wedding present," she told Jack when they entered their house. "It's located in your bedchamber."

They lit a candle and began to mount the stairs. On the top storey, she led him down the corridor to the last room, his bedchamber. It was swathed in red velvet. "I know it's not easy to see at night." She moved to the chimneypiece and held up the candle to illuminate the portrait of Warrior.

"By Jove! It's my horse!" An appreciative smile on his face, he strolled up to the painting. "This is my wedding present?"

She nodded.

"There is nothing that you could have given me that I would have preferred to this—except, of course, your own likeness. I never thought I'd ever be able to afford to have a fine artist like this paint Warrior—and I must tell you, I've often thought of it." He moved to put his arm around her. "Before you, he was my most prized possession."

"Do you really think I hired an expensive artist to paint him?"

"Of course. Look at the realistic quality of the painting."

She could not repress her smile. "Thank you for saying so. I thought it was my best work ever."

"You did not paint this!"

"Indeed I did!"

"I had no notion you were possessed of such talent."

She shrugged. "As I said, it is my best effort. Ever."

He took the candle from her hands, set it upon the chimneypiece, and drew her into his arms. They kissed tenderly. And as the tenderness turned more passionate, she could hardly contain her excitement. Trembling, she drew back and regarded him. "This is our true wedding night, my dearest love. I must go tidy up."

His hand gently caressed her face. "I suppose you'll want to put on a frilly night shift?"

"Oh course! I have been saving an exceedingly expensive one for our wedding night."

"And you'll probably douse yourself with spear mint."

"Naturally."

"Very well. I need to build a fire anyway. I don't want you taking a chill in your already weakened state."

She lit his candle, then went to her bedchamber, which was located next to his. Under Cornelia's guidance, this chamber had been decorated in sky blue and white.

Sitting before her dressing table, she brushed out her bushy head of hair, lamenting that it could not be soft and pretty. For once, she also lamented she had no lady's maid. She would have liked a warm bath. At least the chambermaid had seen to it water was in her basin so she could properly wash.

After brushing out her hair, she began to remove her clothing, then she scrubbed her face first and washed herself all the way to her toes. A good dousing with spear mint left her with a nice, clean scent. She did not admire the heavy floral scents her sisters favored.

Her last act was to put on the practically indecent night shift Cornelia had told her was the very thing to ignite Jack's passions.

She had refrained from telling Cornelia that she was able to ignite Jack's passions without any artifice.

Once she had donned the gown, she peered at herself in the looking glass under the soft light of her candle. How she wished she were a beauty. Sadly, that was not the case.

Fortunately, Jack loved her just the way she was.

Her pulse began to roar in anticipation of what would happen next. She was about to become Jack's wife in every way. Drawing in her breath and picking up the candlestick, she left her room and returned to her husband's.

She eased open the door and softly padded into the chamber. The fire in the hearth of his bedchamber bathed the room in a buttery glow.

Then she heard the unmistakable sound of his heavy, even breathing. Her husband had fallen asleep!

She could not blame him. They had been awake for the past four and twenty hours. She climbed on top his tall tester bed and burrowed herself beneath the coverings, and she, too, quickly fell into a deep slumber.

$\mathcal{C}$hapter 9

The first thing Daphne saw when she awakened the next day was the heavy crimson velvet curtain around the bed. Her husband's bed. The memory that she was in Jack's bed was rather like a bolt of lightning for the way it made her come fully awake. She peered beside her but only saw the crumpled linen where he had lain. Where was her husband? Was she to be rewarded with a glimpse of her Captain Sublime getting clothed?

She sprang up in the bed, her gaze sweeping over the chamber which was now filled with bright sunlight, and their fire had gone cold. Jack was not there. The footed clock on the chimneypiece read four o'clock. It could *not* be four in the afternoon! In her entire life, Daphne had never slept until four in the afternoon. She leapt from the bed.

Then she saw it. Propped on his desk was a sheet of velum. She crossed the room and picked it up. It was a note from her husband.

My dearest, I waited for some time for you to come awake, but you slept so soundly I did not want to wake you. Yesterday was a physically taxing day, especially on one who'd so recently been so sick. You needed your rest in order to get back your strength.

I have gone to give a report on our progress to Lord Castlereagh. Since learning that there was a list, I have renewed hope we shall find it.
Yours, J.

His note left her inordinately sad. Perhaps it wasn't the note. She could not deny that she was disappointed their marriage had yet to be consummated. She could not deny that she was disappointed he hadn't even seen her in her indecent night shift. Nor could she deny that she was disappointed she had been deprived of the sight of her Captain Sublime undressing. He was such a magnificent creature!

Dejected, she returned to her own bedchamber, removed her indecent night shift and carefully folded it for another night, then she quickly dressed. While Jack was out of pocket would be a very good time for her to set in motion a little plan of her own—one she did not want Jack apprised of.

It wasn't that she was deliberately hiding something from him. It was just that she did not want to offend him in any way. And this little plan she'd thought of on the carriage ride home the previous evening/morning would be better executed without Jack's knowledge.

She hurried from the house and after walking a few blocks was able to hire a hackney. She instructed the driver to take her to Whitehall. Her papa would have apoplexy if he knew his daughter was riding through London in a rented hack, but only one other person ever need know what she was doing this afternoon.

As she drove to where the seat of British government was located, she thought of her sister

Virginia's husband, Sir Ronald. He was just the one to help her, but they both would have to be most discreet. Neither Virginia nor Jack could ever learn that Daphne was sharing her information with Sir Ronald.

There was the fact Sir Ronald Johnson was completely trustworthy. He was an undersecretary in Lord Castlereagh's office, and most men in government felt sure he would succeed Castlereagh as Foreign Secretary when that man was elevated to prime minister, which no one doubted would eventually happen.

Sir Ronald was nearly as handsome as Jack, but in Daphne's opinion fell quite short of her husband. The two men were both tall, and now that she thought about it, she realized they were built remarkably alike.

Unlike her Jack, though, Sir Ronald hailed from an old, well-to-do English family. He'd gone to the best schools and belonged to the best clubs.

Which is exactly why Daphne needed him and exactly why Jack could not know she needed Sir Ronald.

The trick was to keep Jack from seeing her, since he, too, was in Whitehall, and he was actually meeting with the only man (besides the king or Regent) who Sir Ronald must answer to. While her hackney coach was crossing the Capital's busy streets at a sound clip, she managed to—not without badly staining her gloves with ink—jot a note for Sir Ronald.

When they arrived at the building where the Foreign Office was located, she instructed her driver to deliver the note to Sir Ronald Johnson. The vague note merely asked that the baronet meet her in front of the building, telling him that she would await him within a hackney coach.

A few minutes later, puzzlement clouding his face, Sir Ronald threw open the door of Daphne's conveyance. "Lady Daphne? How can I be of assistance to you? Are you quite all right?"

"Yes, I am. Perfectly all right. Please, my dear man, do get in the carriage with me."

He regarded her from beneath lowered brows as he climbed in. "When did you return from Spain?"

"Yesterday."

"Astonishingly hasty trip." He folded his long legs into the coach, taking a seat across from her, his brows still lowered.

"Indeed, it was."

"And where is Captain Dryden?"

"Actually, I believe he's in the building you've just left. He needed to speak with Lord Castlereagh. I particularly did not wish for him to see me speaking with you."

"Pray, my lady, why?"

"You'll understand, I think, when I tell you why I needed to speak with you." She drew a fortifying breath. "First I need to impart some things to you that must never be acknowledged to anyone. One of them has to do with the security of England, the other with the good name of your wife's twin."

His eyes rounded.

"Allow me to tell you of the threat to England first. You may or may not be aware of the fact my husband is working with your superior, Lord Castlereagh, regarding a matter of espionage."

"I am privy to some of that information, yes. You must understand I am not at liberty to discuss these matters with you or anyone."

"This afternoon my husband will have informed the Foreign Secretary that we were able to determine that Captain Heffington did, indeed, pass on the list, and it has been traced to London." She told him everything she and Jack had discovered on the previous night. "So, you see, we are almost certain the unfortunate Mr. Prufoy was slain by someone who must have gotten that list. The exciting thing to us is that the murderer may not know the significance of the list—that is, if his aim was to get the letters with which to blackmail."

"A fine piece of deductive work you and the captain have done, but you must enlighten me about the blackmail."

"Actually, I was getting to that. I would like you to do a bit of deduction for us."

He gave her a quizzing look. "Anything you ask, my lady."

"Since you are so very well acquainted with men of the *ton*, I thought you would be the very person to help us learn what man has suddenly come into a large sum of money. I believe he's a man of fashion who was a bit down on his luck but has suddenly become flush with funds."

"I'm afraid you've rather lost me. Why is the man with the list suddenly flush with money? Have you knowledge he's sold it to the French?"

"No." She gathered her thoughts a moment before proceeding. "That's the other clandestine matter, the other thing you must never repeat."

"What is?" He looked bewildered.

"The man who possesses the list is also in possession of love letters that belonged to Major Styles at the time of his death."

He nodded, and his eyes lighted with recognition. "I see now. These letters must have been written by my wife's twin."

"Precisely. And Cornelia specifically did not want Virginia to know of their existence."

"Because my dear wife does not approve of infidelity."

"Exactly."

"And I must also deduce that my wife's twin has been paying exorbitant sums to a blackmailer who holds these letters?"

"You are brilliant!"

"Therefore you wish for me to frequently patronize the clubs to which I belong, keeping my eyes and ears open to learn if a fellow member has recently come into money."

"That is exactly what I wish!"

He nodded thoughtfully. "Now I understand why you did not want your captain to know about our meeting."

She nodded. "He belongs to no clubs, nor does he desire to. It all comes down to that disparity in our stations that seems to bother him." She paused a moment. "As to the business with Cornelia's letters, I beg that you never mention them to Virginia. Cornelia most especially did not want her to know. And I don't suppose I need to stress to you that my husband is not to know this meeting between us took place?"

* * *

As Jack left his very satisfactory meeting with Lord Castlereagh, he could not purge from his mind the vision of his wife lying beside him, in his bed, that morning. He had allowed himself to stare at her bare flesh until he became uncommonly heated. Where in the devil had she found so indecent a night shift? The duchess must have had a hand in selecting the skimpy piece of fragile lace.

This was one time he did not object to the duchess's interference.

He thought he had never seen anything lovelier than his bride with the mellow morning sun bathing her fair slenderness. Her extraordinarily thick hair fanned across the pillows, and her night shift offered him a tantalizing glimpse of her little breasts, which made it most difficult for him to allow her to continue sleeping.

But when he remembered how wretchedly sick she had been on the ship, he knew there was no power on earth that would allow him to awaken her. She needed to regain her good health—though she was loathe to admit to even the least infirmity.

Late that afternoon, as he was skipping down the steps from the Foreign Office to the Strand, he got a glimpse of Sir Ronald. It was no surprise seeing his brother-in-law at the Foreign Office. He was, after all, undersecretary to Lord Castlereagh. What was surprising, though, was the fact his wealthy kinsmen would be entering a common hackney coach.

As he watched Sir Ronald, Jack got a glimpse of the woman in the hack. A woman who was not Sir Ronald's wife. A woman with wildly aggressive golden-brownish curls. A woman who looked suspiciously like Jack's very own wife.

What in the devil would Daphne be doing in a hack? And why in the devil would she be so clandestinely meeting with Sir Ronald?

* * *

Despite his conviction that it had been his wife in the hackney coach secretly meeting with Sir Ronald, Jack had allowed himself to hope he had been wrong. But when he saw Daphne returning to their home in the rented hack a half hour later, his stomach plummeted.

He swung open the front door to greet her with a scowl. "I did not know Lady Daphne patronized hackneys."

Lifting her skirts, she raced up the front steps and brushed a kiss on his cheek. "But, my darling, you had taken off in our carriage—which reminds me, don't you think we should perhaps hire it for another day?"

He shrugged. "What with paying the livery fees, this is costing us a great deal of money."

They strolled to the drawing room.

"I had no notion how expensive renting a hack could be."

Though he wanted to ask what necessitated her having to rent the public conveyance, he would be patient and wait for her to satisfy his curiosity. "Perhaps we should reconsider getting our own carriage."

She pursed her lips. "It's a pity we don't live closer to my parents. If we did, we could use their mews and their grooms."

"And have your parents feed Andy, too?" He scowled. "It's a great deal cheaper to pay livery stables than to purchase a house closer to your parents."

"We are fortunate that Mama gave us this one." She linked her arm through his. "Do you like the house?"

He peered down into her face. He could see his reflection in her spectacles. "It's a lovely house, and we are very fortunate. You will not be happy to learn, though, that our lone servant has been called away."

Daphne's brows lowered. "I hope it's not something terrible."

"I'm afraid her mother is gravely ill."

"Poor dear." She gazed up into his face. "We are so blessed. You and me."

When was she going to tell him about her meeting with Sir Ronald?

"Come and sit beside me on the sofa and tell me about your meeting with Lord Castlereagh."

The faded green silk sofa thy sat on was situated near the hearth, but there was no fire. "His lordship was happy that we had made so much progress, and he was gratified that we determined that Heffington's list must have made it to London."

"So far, our guesses have been rather brilliant."

His brows lowered.

"I cannot use that word even when it is just the two of us?"

"A man's accomplishments should speak for themselves."

"I don't suppose a wife should gush about her husband's successes, but if others want to praise you, I see nothing wrong with that." She shrugged. "Allow me to change the topic of our conversation. I only thought of it this morning, but I thought perhaps it might be significant."

"What might be significant?"

"We know that Mr. Prufoy—who does sound like a remarkably noble fellow—delivered the major's things to his widow."

He nodded, his brows hitched.

"Because we have learned that Mr. Prufoy was so incredibly admirable that he would not even sully my sister's name—and God knows she deserved it—it is highly unlikely he would ever have told other men that he was in possession of Cornelia's torrid letters."

"I agree, but I don't see what you're getting at."

"What I'm getting at is that it just may be possible that when Mr. Prufoy was returning the dead major's things to the widow, perhaps someone else was paying his condolences—someone who knew about the major's adultery with my sister—and this disreputable person who must have been in need of money ascertained that Mr. Prufoy might be in possession of those letters which could be worth a great deal of money."

Now *she* really was being brilliant! "There's one way we can find out."

Her countenance brightened. "I can ask Mrs. Styles!"

"Perhaps I should."

"Because you supposedly served with her husband?"

"I won't actually lie."

She cupped her hand into his cheek. "I know you won't."

Why could his wife not be as honest as he? Her little prevarications never hurt anyone, but they could be most vexing. He was reminded of the time she told her father Jack could speak Hottentot but had neglected to tell Jack.

Why had she not disclosed to him that she had secretly met with Sir Ronald?

"Now, Lady Daphne," he said, his voice stern, "I would like to know where you went in the hack."

And what in the bloody hell were you doing with Sir Ronald?

She did not answer for several seconds. "I went to my father's solicitor. He's outrageously clever about procuring the most capable staff imaginable."

His hopes sank. Was she not going to admit to meeting Sir Ronald? "Then we will soon have servants to light our fires and answer our door?"

She shrugged. "I don't know how soon. These things take time. I think you completely agree that we had to wait until we returned from Spain to hire staff?"

"Of course. We had no way of knowing our return would be as quick as it was." He wondered if he should just come right out and ask her what she was doing inside that coach with Sir Ronald. Now, if Sir Ronald had resembled the duchess's short, portly, bald-headed duke, Jack would not have gotten his hackles up, but Sir Ronald was acknowledged to be the most handsome man in the *ton.*

And Jack did not like his wife sitting within the intimacy of a hired hack with that damned baronet!

"And where else did you go?" he asked.

"I wanted to get back to my husband as quickly as possible."

He felt sick. She was lying. He got to his feet.

"What are you doing?"

He was so angry he could shake her. They had been married not quite a week, and already she was lying to him. What kind of foundation was this upon which to build a solid marriage? Yet, if he questioned her and became accusatory, he would be culpable in destroying the trust which should be the backbone of a good marriage. "I'm going to visit Style's widow."

"At least let me give you the direction." There was impatience and something else—veiled anger?—in her voice.

He had best get out of there before he exploded.

* * *

His wife's description of the widow had been most accurate. What he had not counted upon was his own shame. God, but he hated to lie! And while he had not exactly told Mrs. Styles he had known her husband, he had allowed her to believe they were acquainted.

The two of them had sat there in her drawing room, hatchments heavy over her windows, as they spoke of her dead husband. "It's a terrible pity that now his batman is dead, too," Jack said.

"Indeed it was! I had just seen him the day before he died."

"Would that have been when he was returning your husband's things to you?"

She nodded solemnly and dabbed at her eyes with the handkerchief she kept in her hand. "Prufoy was devoted to my husband."

"From all accounts he was a very fine batman."

"My husband often said Prufoy was the finest batman ever to serve."

"It is most difficult to come by a good batman. In that your husband was fortunate."

"That's exactly what Lord Lambeth told Prufoy that day."

Jack's pulse accelerated. Daphne's hunch was right! The culprit *had* been visiting the widow on the day Prufoy returned her husband's effects. Fanny Hale had told them Prufoy was to deliver the list to a lord. Lord Lambeth must be Prufoy's murderer and the duchess's blackmailer!

His brows elevated. "The day Prufoy brought your husband's things?"

"Yes. Lord Lambeth was my husband's greatest friend." She shrugged. "He was ever so kind in expressing his condolences. It made me regret that I had not always held the viscount in great affection. I often blamed him for keeping my husband away from me, for keeping him in the clubs where both of them lost more at play than they should have."

Bulls eye! He could not believe he and Daphne had been back in London but one day, and they had already determined who possessed the list. Not *they* precisely. Daphne had done a damned good job of analysis.

And, damn but he was angry with her!

He thanked the widow for seeing him and took his leave. Each minute he was away from Daphne his fury increased. Why was she deliberately deceiving him? In the mood he was in, he was apt to start a terrible row with her.

Not far from Mrs. Styles' he saw the swaying red and white sign for the White Lion public house. He was just mad enough to get stinking drunk, but of course he wouldn't. A bumper of ale might serve to calm him.

As he entered the White Lion, he sensed that he was being followed. He strode to the bar, and just as he was about to speak, an unkempt man of his own age ambled up beside him. "I have something for you from an old friend."

Jack whirled to face him and saw that he was missing a front tooth—just before the man's fist came crashing into Jack's face. It came so unexpectedly, Jack was not able to brace himself but went falling back.

Then from the other side, two more men of similar age, build, and shabby clothing closed around Jack and began to pummel him with their fists. Three against one.

And one of the men had a knife.

$\mathcal{C}$hapter 10

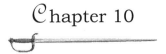

The fragment of light that penetrated his darkness grew brighter until he began to realize he was not dead after all. He became conscious of voices. Daphne's. Which made him happy. Then Sir Ronald's deep voice intruded with the discordance of a shrieking cat at a harp recital and made him doubly conscious of how bloody, bloody bad off he was. He understood what it felt like to be cannon fodder.

He was quite certain his ribs had been shattered because his meager effort at moving sent a surging pain the length of his trunk, and each breath he took was like the stab of a knife. His throbbing head felt twice the size of normal. And his hands! God, but he'd fought for his life. It was some consolation in his misery to know he had given almost as good as he got.

Or as bad as he got. Had it been an even fight, Jack knew he would have been standing now, not lying there like a helpless woman.

Before Jack could attempt to integrate into the rest of his world, he wanted to remember. Remember what? What was his last memory? Anger. Daphne had lied to him. He'd left her. There was another woman. . . oh, yes. He'd met with Major Styles' widow. Then what? The tavern!

His last recollection was those three men closing around him as threatening as a noose. His hands fisted at the memory. Just like with Prufoy, it hadn't been a tavern brawl. It had been a deliberate attempt to do murder.

"Oh, look, Ronnie! He's moved."

It was his wife's excited voice. And she had called that womanizing rake *Ronnie*! Jack fleetingly wished it had been Sir Ronald's handsome face that had been beaten to a pulp at that damned public house.

As long as that man was wherever it was they were, Jack had no desire to talk to either of them. Or to open his eyes. Then something occurred which sliced through his resolve as easily as the severing of Sampson's hair.

He heard Daphne cry.

And all he could think of was reassuring her.

His eyes came fully open. Nothing had ever looked lovelier to him than the sight of Daphne standing there, her eyes red from crying. Over him. As he peered at her, he suddenly realized she was not wearing her spectacles. Was she attempting to make herself lovelier for Sir Ronald? "Where are your spectacles, madam?" Jack asked, his voice icy. Calling her madam did give him a heady sense of possession. And it reminded that damned baronet that she was a married woman.

She pulled her spectacles from a pocket in her skirt, put them on, and offered him a feeble smile. Then she came to sit on the side of the bed and gently stroke his face, her tears still gathering until they spilled down her cheeks. "How are you, my dearest?"

"Bloody awful."

"We had the physician here. He seems to think you've escaped fatal injuries to your lungs or heart. Tell me what hurts."

"It would be easier to tell you what doesn't." He still refused to look at that lecher who was married to his wife's sister.

"Are you aware that it has been almost four and twenty hours since I last saw you?" Daphne asked.

Good God! How long had he been unconscious? He shook his head . . . and wished he hadn't. Even the slightest movement hurt.

"'Twas the worst night of my four and twenty years."

It served her right. It was all her fault. He would never have stopped at that public house had she not infuriated him with her lies. It would have been her just desserts if he'd bloody well been killed!

"When Cornelia and Virginia were little, one of them could always tell if something happened to the other, even when they were not near each other. I understand that now. I knew when you did not return home in a timely fashion last night that something terrible had befallen you." Her voice broke, and she began to sob.

How could he stay angry with her? He reached for her hand . . . even if it did cause him considerable pain. "There, there. I am here now, and that's all that matters."

"Would it hurt you if I try to embrace you?" Her voice had a girl-like quality about it.

"Let's see." They would show that Sir Ronald!

She eased close to him, ever so gently, and did not elicit even a wince. When he went to put an arm around her, he discovered he could not.

"Does it hurt?" she asked.

He nodded.

She pressed her lips to his forehead.

"How did I get here?"

"Sir Ronald brought you."

To Jack's bedchamber on the top floor of their townhouse? It would have been no easy feat to lug a man who weighed fifteen stone up two flights of steep stairs. Jack stiffened, and grudgingly allowed himself to make eye contact with the tall, way-too-masculine looking man. Jack inclined his head. "I am obliged." That was the most he could manage toward the blasted rake.

"When you did not return, I was half out of my mind." Daphne said. "I couldn't leave the house because I wanted to be here if you should return, if you should need me." She shrugged, her voice hitching. "I finally had enough presence of mind to get a street urchin to deliver a note to Sir Ronald."

The baronet moved closer to Jack's velvet-draped bed. "I came straight away. Lady Daphne gave me Mrs. Styles' address, so I went to question her. She told me you'd left before dark."

"He came back and told me," Daphne said, stroking her husband's hair. "I was able to convince Sir Ronald that you must have met with foul play between here and Mrs. Styles' house. He obliged me by investigating every possible diversion."

"It was nearly midnight when I found you at the White Lion."

"Were the men who attacked me still there?"

Sir Ronald shook his head ruefully. "The proprietor said he'd never seen them before. Apparently he and some other patrons were able to get them off of you before they succeeded in killing you. The three of them then fled." Sir Ronald paused. "The men at the White Lion said you'd put up the most valiant fight they had ever seen. You left your three assailants half crippled and hobbling away from the establishment."

Though normally a modest man who disliked any reference to his skills, just this once he rather relished such a narration in front of his wife.

"Which came as no surprise to me." Daphne beamed at Jack. Then her voice turned serious. "You know, my dearest, you may have been right about the duc d'Arblier being in London."

Her words were like a blow to his windpipe. Of course he'd been right! The duc wanted Jack out of the way. Did that mean the duc wanted to be sure he got the list before Jack? If that were the case, then it wasn't too late.

As wretched as he felt, his wife did something that made him forget the maddening pain. She lifted his hand and pressed nibbly kisses into his palm.

Their eyes met and held. And he knew she was deeply in love with him.

"Can you tell me what you learned?" she asked sweetly, then her gaze skipped to her brother-in-law. "Since Sir Ronald *is* the first undersecretary to Lord Castlereagh, he is acquainted with our mission, and I've had to apprise him of what we've been doing."

Jack met his wife's quizzing gaze and nodded. "You were right."

Her (still reddened) eyes widened. "About Mr. Prufoy meeting one of the major's friends at the widow's house?"

"Yes."

She waited for a moment. "Well, who was it?"

He most certainly did not want to tell her as long as Sir Ronald was in the room.

Give the man his due. Sir Ronald had the goodness to clear his throat and say, "Dear me, I'd best be on my way. Or my wife will become as hysterical as you were last night, Lady Daphne. Daresay it's a Sidworth family trait."

Hysterical? His Daphne? Because of him? While news of his wife's distress would normally not be balm to his wounds, on this day it was.

She spun around to face the baronet. "I am destitute of words to thank you for all you've done for us."

"It was nothing."

Carrying a man who weighed fifteen stone up two flights of stairs certainly was something! The arrogant man was fishing for a compliment from Daphne, and Jack prayed she would not play to his vanity.

"Why, you carried my husband to this room with no assistance. You were wonderful!"

Jack was destitute of words for the man, too. Did that cocky Sir Ronald Johnson have to single-handedly haul Jack into the house? No doubt it was a ploy to display his uncommon strength. The man was already noted for being a talented pugilist as well as a skilled swordsman. Had he no modesty?

Jack would wager he'd swaggered when he carried him up to the third floor!

Good manners, though, demanded that Jack express his gratitude. "Good of you to see me home."

"Think nothing of it, my dear fellow. I shall talk to Lord Castlereagh to see it he's heard any reports about d'Arblier being in London."

After Daphne walked Sir Ronald to the door, she came back and sat on his bed, drawing his hand into hers. "Do I know the man?"

She was entirely too curious. "What man?"

"You know very well what man! The one who was at Mrs. Styles' house when Mr. Prufoy brought her husband's things."

"Oh, that man. How am I to know if you know him?"

"What is his name?"

"Apparently he's some kind aristocrat because he's a Lord Something or Other." He loved leading her on.

Her brows elevated. "Lord Who?" She made no effort to conceal her impatience.

He remembered very well the man's name—despite all that he'd been through since the moment the name had been emblazoned upon his memory—but he was going to tease her a bit more.

She deserved that. And more. Why in the devil had she lied to him? And why in the blazes was she meeting that rogue Sir Ronald inside a hired hack?

"Let me think," he said. "The man's name reminded me of a place."

"Russell? Like Russell Square?"

He pursed his lips. "No. Not Russell."

"I don't suppose you've ever met the man?"

"No. Never heard of the fellow."

"What about Kent?"

"Not a county, either. Of that I'm certain."

She leaned back and regarded him through narrowed eyes. "Captain Jack Dryden, I do believe you are pulling my leg! Even with multiple injuries, I know how sharp your mind is. You would never forget something as important as the identity of a . . . a murderer."

His wife knew him entirely too well. He was incapable of repressing a slight smile that tweaked at his lips. "Lambeth."

She gasped. "Lord Lambeth?"

He went to nod, then knew it would be entirely too painful to do so. "Indeed. Do you know him?"

"I've never met him. I believe he's between my age and that of my parents."

"I don't suppose he has a post in government?"

"Not that I know of."

Jack went to purse his lips, but such an act reopened a cut and hurt like the devil. "I'll wager the man's a murderer."

"Yes, it would seem so." Her brows lowered. "But why did you say his name was a place? I don't know any town or square—Oh yes! You were thinking of Lambeth Palace."

"One of the most important residences in London."

"I suppose the Archbishop of Canterbury would be in perfect agreement."

She was lost in thought for a moment, then offered her opinion on Lord Lambeth. "The way I see it, when Lord Lambeth saw Mr. Prufoy at the widow's—where he'd come to express condolences—he realized the batman had the major's things and because Lord Lambeth was close to the major—the two men would be of the same age—he knew about his affair with my sister and likely knew of the letters."

"Mrs. Styles did tell me her husband and Lord Lambeth were the closest of friends. If the peer was in need of money—the widow indicated he lured her husband into gambling—he had to know letters from a duchess would be extremely valuable."

"As, indeed, they were. I don't understand why he had to kill the poor batman, though. Why could he not have just gone to the man's rooms when he was not there?"

"I have never understood the workings of a murderer's mind."

"I wonder if he knows the importance of Captain Heffington's list?"

"A pity we don't know a single name that was on it."

His eyes narrowed. That slight movement hurt like hell. "You did not tell that damned Sir Ronald about the duchess's letters, did you?"

"How could I? You specifically told me not to tell another soul. And why do you refer to that sweet man as *damned*?"

"Sweet man, my elbow," he muttered. Jack was not about to admit that the baronet was tall and handsome. Especially not to his wife. "He's a womanizing rake."

She put hands to waist, stiffened, and looked askance at him. "Only that one indiscretion, to my knowledge. He and Virginia are quite happily married, and as Cornelia says—not without jealousy—*disgustingly besotted over one another.*"

"Enough talk of that man. What next, Madam Schemer?"

"We get you well."

"On the third day I shall be good as new." He did not believe his own words. "What is your true opinion about the men who tried to kill me?"

"I believe the duc d'Arblier's back in London. You must own, the very method of the attack on you sounds like the underhanded, vile kind of thing he would orchestrate. He obviously hired the worst sort of murderers to do you in—to get you out of the way because he knows you will spoil his evil plans."

"It does seem plausible that d'Arblier's back, but my attackers did not speak French."

"The duc has the resources to hire cutthroats. Perhaps Lord Castlereagh may know if the duc has managed to steal into our country."

A bell sounded.

Her gaze leapt to his. "Oh, dear, that's the front door."

"In the absence of servants, may I suggest you get the door? I am aware that the daughter of an earl is unused to such a task."

"I keep forgetting we have no servants!" She tore out of the chamber and raced down the stairs.

A moment later she returned with Fanny Hale.

"Oh, my dearest," Daphne exclaimed, "she has remembered the name of the nobleman who Mr. Prufoy wished to contact!"

$\mathcal{C}$hapter 11

"My dear Mrs. Hale!" Daphne had exclaimed when she opened the door to the woman. "Do come in. Where are your children? I assure you they would have been perfectly welcome here. "

"Thank you, my lady. Me eldest boy is most capable of looking after the younger ones," the woman said as she entered the house, "but I thank you for your kindness in extending the invitation to them."

"Please excuse the chaos here. My husband and I are just back from Spain and haven't yet had the opportunity to procure a full staff of servants." She ran her eye over the youngish mother. Fanny Hale had obviously made every effort to dress in her Sunday finest for a visit to an aristocrat's home. She wore a serviceable frock of dark gray bombazine with snow white gloves, and a white collar. She not only looked spotless, she smelled like a rose. Daphne was ashamed of herself for suspecting that Fanny Hale could ever have been a prostitute.

At the narrow staircase, Daphne put her hand on the banister, then turned back to Mrs. Hale. "Your visit will cheer my husband. I regret to say he's met with a rather unfortunate accident. Well, actually it wasn't an accident. I believe someone—

possibly the same person who murdered your Mr. Prufoy—wished to kill my husband."

Mrs. Hale's hand flew to her mouth as she let out a little yelp. "How dreadful!"

"Not nearly as dreadful as what you've have to endure," Daphne said, tenderly setting her hand to the woman's forearm. "I am blessed to still have my Jack."

The other woman's eyes misted.

"Have you remembered the lord's name?" Daphne asked.

"I 'ave."

"Come, let's go tell my husband. I know your visit will hasten his recovery." Though Daphne was inordinately curious to know of the mysterious lord, she would wait until they reached Jack's bedchamber.

When Mrs. Hale entered his room, Jack attempted to sit up, but the movement caused him to wince and collapse back into the bed pillows.

Daphne came to sit beside him. "Mrs. Hale has remembered the lord's name." She turned from Jack to face the dead batman's lover. "Pray, who is the lord your Mr. Prufoy was going to see?"

"I knew I would know the aristocrat's name if I heard it, but it weren't a common name, if you understand me?"

Daphne nodded. Would the poor woman please just tell them the name!

"I heard my cousin—who's in service with a fine gentleman—say her gentleman has a book in his library what listed all the lords and ladies; so, I went to her gentleman's house to see the book." She flashed Daphne a bright smile. "Me mum was well educated and taught all of us to read and write."

Many of those who were in service at her parents' house, Daphne knew, could not read and write.

"The gentleman was ever so nice about allowing me to use his library when I said I was assisting Lady Daphne Dryden. I looked up and down the pages until I recognized the name." She paused for dramatic effect. "It was Lord Braithwite."

Daphne gasped, her gaze darting to Jack.

His brows lowered. "At the admiralty?"

Mrs. Hale nodded. "The gentleman, whose name is Mr. Ashworth, said his book was the newest edition 'cause his wife likes to keep up with the nobility. According to the book, Lord Braithwite is some kind of Lord of the Admiralty."

"You, Mrs. Hale, have been enormously helpful," Jack said. "Pray, love, you must compensate the lady for giving us so much of her time."

"That's a very good idea." Daphne faced Fanny Hale. "There's one other question I wish to ask."

"Yes, my lady?"

"Did you go to Mr. Prufoy's rooms after his death? You had every right to, being the person he was closest to on earth." Daphne met her husband's gaze. "I cannot believe we did not think of this sooner. Just because we know the wicked person responsible for his death went there to steal the papers should not have precluded us from looking there."

"My wife is correct once more."

Fanny Hale fairly cowered, her pale blue eyes as frightened as a terrified child's.

Daphne rushed to take her hand. "My dear Fanny, if you took something—anything—from Mr. Prufoy's lodgings, do not be embarrassed to admit it. It's the very thing your dear man would have wanted. It is just that we are looking for some papers that are very important to the British government—papers we believe were in Mr. Prufoy's possession—and we must see that they don't get into the hands of the French."

The other woman's eyes widened. "I didn't take no papers."

"Do you have a key to his place?"

Fanny nodded, patting her frayed reticule. "I do. He was paid up 'till next month."

Daphne turned to Jack. "We will need to search, even though we know the murderer got those letters."

He gave a fatigued sigh. "We?"

"Perhaps Mrs. Hale could come with me."

He scowled. "You need a man to protect you."

"Then I shall ask Sir Ronald."

"You will not!"

Daphne looked perplexed. "I do wish you wouldn't be so beastly about Sir Ronald. He's terribly nice."

"And I do wish you'd not keep the man in your pocket. Can you not get one of your father's footmen or postillions or such to accompany you?"

"Very well, though I cannot like leaving you alone."

"Nobody would dare come here in broad daylight."

"You do have a point there."

* * *

Daphne had the devil of a time getting away from her parents' house with the pair of burly footmen. Lord and Lady Sidworth were unaware that she had returned from Spain and were full of questions about her trip and about why she had need of footmen for so short a period of time. She gave vague answers about moving furniture at the new house. Before she raced off, she implored her mother to assist in procuring servants. That should keep her ladyship busy. Lady Sidworth was happiest when she thought she was helping others.

Back in the carriage headed for Cotton Lane, Daphne turned to her companion. It had suddenly occurred to her that she had omitted to tell Fanny Hale about her lover's dying words. "Have you wondered how we learned of your existence?"

"Yes, my lady. I was going to ask you about that."

"From the Cock & Stalk we learned the name of the surgeon who treated Mr. Prufoy when he was dying."

A sob broke from the other woman. "Was it my name what was on his lips when he . . . died?" She barely got the words out when her tears gushed, and her sobs strengthened.

Even though Daphne had never met Prufoy, she, too, began to weep as she nodded and hugged the crying woman beside her.

They could have gotten to Cotton Lane faster on foot. The streets were teeming with all manner of conveyances. A donkey-cart piled high with turnips trudged along slowly in front of them. Coming abreast of them in the opposite direction was a fine coach pulled by four matched bays. The gold printing on its jet black door proclaimed the coach the property of Richard Rowland. Windsor.

After that, a hackney coach, followed by a wagon of coal, and after that, another hackney.

Not far from the Cock & Stalk, their carriage halted, and the women got out. Daphne much preferred entering Cotton Lane in the daytime. It was no longer menacing as it had been when she was there two nights previously. The knowledge that one man had been murdered and Jack almost murdered—both of these men trained soldiers—sent her back to the carriage to request the footmen accompany them.

"When you came here after Mr. Prufoy died," Daphne said to Mrs. Hale when they entered Cotton Lane, "did his lodgings look as if someone had been there? Someone looking for something?"

"Indeed they did, but I thought it be the army people because my Mr. Prufoy had told me he had papers that might be important."

"Do you know where he kept them?"

She nodded. "In his Bible. And there was nothing there when I arrived."

Daphne found herself wondering why Prufoy had been murdered in a public house when the dark, little-traveled Cotton Lane was so much more secluded. The only explanation that made any sense was that the murderer wanted the death to look like a typical tavern brawl.

Not premeditated murder.

He must have wished to avoid an investigation a murder may have necessitated.

Mrs. Hale came to stand before the weathered door and drew a deep breath, fetched the key, and opened the door. Daphne's heart went out to the poor woman who must be remembering the happy times she'd had there with her Mr. Prufoy.

Before Daphne stepped into the narrow little house, she faced the footmen. "I merely require that you men stand at watch." She favored them with a smile. "I'm thinking you'll be like the soldiers who guard the Princess of Wales' house—though I daresay that will require a great deal of imagination!"

The closest to her cracked a grin.

The small, musty room they entered was so dark, they could hardly see anything. Daphne strode to the window, pulled back the dark, heavy curtains and opened the casements. "Perhaps the fresh air will help remove the staleness."

The two women, silent as in church, surveyed the chamber. Even the servants' rooms at Daphne's modest new house were larger than this. A narrow stairway hugged against the side wall that was papered in a floral pattern which had almost been obscured from decades of burning coal fires. Her glance fell to the narrow chimneypiece, cold now these past several weeks. A handful of cooking implements hung from wall hooks near the hearth, and a scrubbed oak table was also near. Daphne suspected it served as desk as well as dining table. Half of the table held a small stack of books—including the dog-eared Bible—and the other half held two glasses, two cups, and two plates.

Daphne glanced around the rest of the chamber. There was one wooden chair tucked under the table, and an upholstered chair was the only other piece in the room.

She went to the books and began to flip through the pages. "I'm assuming you tidied the room when you came?"

Mrs. Hale nodded. "Me dear Mr. Prufoy was neat as a pin. I didn't like to leave his things messy like those wicked men left them."

In addition to the Bible, there was a well-read copy of *Robinson Crusoe*, a volume of Thomas Gray's poetry, and a religious tract written by Hannah More. How sad. The small stack comprised one man's personal library. Daphne held each book upside down and shook, but not even a scrap of paper came loose.

His possessions had been so meager, there were not a lot of hiding places, which was understandable, given that the man had spent much of his life following the drum. "How old was Mr. Prufoy?"

"He would have turned forty next year."

More than half his life must have been spent in military service. Daphne nodded thoughtfully. "Shall we go upstairs?"

Mrs. Hale looked as if she were glued to the dusty wooden floor. "If it's all the same to you, I would rather not. That was a special place I only went with the man I adored."

How utterly heartbreaking! Daphne started climbing the stairs. Each time her slipper touched the tread, the sagging wood creaked. In happier times the two lovers would have ascended the steps, hand in hand. Daphne could have wept for the poor woman's profound loss. She would have given every guinea she possessed if it could have restored Mr. Prufoy to Fanny Hale.

The stairs terminated in another small chamber, exactly the size of the one below it. A wobbly railing separated the bedchamber from the stairwell. The first thing she did was stride to the window and open the heavy woolen curtains to allow light into the room. Her gaze circled the chamber. Eli Prufoy's uniform hung on wall pegs just as he must have left it, just as if it were awaiting his return. Daphne's eyes filled with tears.

Her gaze moved to the bed, which took up most of the chamber. Just as Fanny Hale said, its coverings were perfectly straightened, not a single wrinkle or bulge. It was there where the two lovers had been so happy in each others' arms.

Daphne's heart caught at the thought of lying with Jack—and at so many touching emotions: powerful love, gratitude that his life had been spared, and now, worry. She needed to hurry back to him.

A quick search of the man's pockets revealed nothing. Then she took off the bed coverings, searching for anything out of the ordinary. She looked beneath the straw mattress, but nothing was there, either. After she was convinced the room contained no papers, she went to put the linens back upon the bed, and it suddenly occurred to her she had no notion of how to make a bed. It was not something an earl's daughter ever need learn.

Knowing that Fanny Hale was not likely to return there and see her dear, tidy Mr. Prufoy's bed in a so disheveled a state, Daphne turned her back on it and started back down the stairs.

"My dear Mrs. Hale, I don't believe there are any important papers in these rooms. Tell me, when you came here after you learned of his death, were you able to determine if anything was missing?"

"Just the papers what he kept in the Bible. Nothing else seemed to be missing."

"The question I'm going to ask you next is not intended to accuse you of any wrongdoing, but I need to know everything you took away on the day you came."

The two women's eyes locked.

"I knew where he kept money. In his boot. It came to fourteen guineas."

"I am certain—as you are—that he would have wanted you to have the money." Daphne's eyes locked again with Fanny's. "Anything else?"

The woman nodded solemnly. "I unpinned this from his uniform." She fingered a regimental pin attached to her dress. Were Daphne more discerning about clothing, she would have noticed it before now. But, of course, she was hopelessly unfashionable.

"I wear it always."

Just as Daphne would never remove the gold band Jack had placed on her hand their wedding day. "I think we've seen enough." Her voice cracked. Her melancholy thoughts kept reverting to the previous night, to the terrifying site of Sir Ronald carrying Jack's lifeless body into their house. She had to rush home and make certain Jack had not taken a turn for the worse.

They left the chambers, and Mrs. Hale locked the door behind them.

It then occurred to Daphne that someone who lived in this quiet little court may have seen the murderer enter or leave Eli Prufoy's lodgings. "I beg that you wait a moment while I knock upon the neighbors' doors."

The next-door-neighbor to the south was an elderly woman who apparently lived alone. "I'm inquiring about the chambers next to yours," Daphne said, pointing toward Eli Prufoy's. "Did you see someone other than the resident enter those chambers?"

As wrinkled as a prune drying in the sun, the white-haired woman nodded. "He died. Killed at the Cock & Stalk."

So she was hard of hearing. "Yes, I know. Did you see another man—or possibly more than one—enter his chambers?" This time Daphne nearly shouted.

The woman shook her head. "I never leave me chambers. Me daughter brings me food twice a week."

As deaf as she was, the murderer could have bludgeoned Prufoy to death in the next house, and this woman would not have been able to hear a thing. Daphne smiled and took her leave.

The house on the north side of Prufoy's was where the two lads lived who had initially told Daphne and Jack about Prufoy's murder. The eldest of the two looked to be eight or nine while the youngest was no more than five. The lads were there, and they remembered Daphne. "You was with that army gent what gave us money!"

"Indeed I was. You are most observant. I have another question for you today. Did you see anyone enter the chambers next door—Mr. Prufoy's—anyone who was not accompanied by Mr. Prufoy?"

The elder boy's gaze leapt to Fanny Hake. "I seen her, but mostly she was with Mr. Prufoy."

"You are wonderfully observant. Exactly the kind of lad I seek," Daphne said. "Did you perchance see a man or more than one man enter the dead man's place?"

He shook his head. "He was quiet like, but ever so nice."

A smile crossed Fanny's face as she nodded her agreement.

The younger boy tugged on his brother's sleeve. "What about that night you heard that noise next door?"

"Stupid. She didn't ask me what I heard. She asked what I seen. I didn't see nothing that night."

"I did," the younger lad said.

$\mathcal{C}$hapter 12

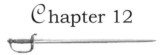

Daphne lowered herself to the younger boy's level. "You saw another man next door?"

He nodded. "Me and Bobby was woke up by a noise, and I looked out the window and seen a man sticking a piece of something like metal to open the door at Mr. Prufoy's. But I was scared he would come after us next, so I hid under the covers."

Knowing how dark that courtyard was at night, Daphne realized there must have been a full moon. Was it the night of Prufoy's death? "Can you tell me what the man looked like?"

He shook his head. "It was late, late at night and dark."

"Could you tell if he was dressed like a rich man or not?"

He shook his head, then brightened. "I remember the moonlight shined on his head. He didn't wear no hat, and his hair was light like mine." The brothers were both blond.

Daphne quizzed the elder. "And you didn't see anything?"

"I was too sleepy to get up."

"Well, I thank both of you for being as helpful as possible." She took pence from her reticule and gave several to each lad before she and Mrs. Hale returned to the carriage.

"I can walk home faster from here than in your carriage, my lady," Fanny Hale said.

"You have been so very helpful and have given us so much of your time, I wish to give you some meager compensation." Daphne took the woman's badly frayed reticule and dumped all the coins in hers into the other woman's.

"That is very kind of you, my lady."

* * *

When she threw open the front door of Dryden House, a strong aroma of onions struck her. The smell permeated the entire house. She knew very well Jack was in no condition to be out of bed. . . Jack! She wouldn't have a second's peace until she reassured herself he was all right. She flew up two flights of stairs and sprinted down the third-floor corridor to the last room.

Lying in the large tester bed, he lay as still as . . .a corpse, and his eyes were closed. Her heart beat prodigiously, and not necessarily from being winded. She approached the bed, terrified because of the eerie silence. Didn't Jack usually snore when he slept? She set a trembling hand on his shoulder. Thank God it was warm!

Her light touch was enough to awaken him, those near-black eyes of his flicking open. "How do you feel?" she asked, tenderly stroking his dark hair.

"Bloody awful, but I'll be out of this bed day after tomorrow."

Even a busted lip and a purple eye socket could not detract from his handsomeness. How she adored looking at his very satisfactory face with its dark, patrician countenance. "We shall see. Dearest? Can you tell me why our home smells of onions?"

"Because we now have a cook."

A smile lifted her face. "How perfectly charming. How did we get one?"

"Your mother brought her. Apparently the girl has been a scullery maid at Sidworth House for two or three years."

"Annie!"

"Yes, as I recall, that is her name—not that I've met her. Your mother said she's been observing their cook. The girl apparently expressed an interest in seeking a position as a cook in a small household."

"How perfect! I do hope Mama inquired about your food preferences?"

He rolled his eyes. "First, I had the devil of a time explaining why I'm in bed looking as I do."

"Oh, dear. I did neglect to tell her about your newest indisposition."

"What do you mean, my *newest* indisposition?" His brows scrunched downward.

"Remember, my parents believe you were suffering from one of those contagious diseases when you were in Brighton. I cannot remember if it was measles or mumps."

"This time it's obviously not a disease."

"So how did you explain your injuries?"

"I didn't have to. The moment she saw me she jumped to her own assumptions—incorrect as they were."

"Oh, dear, I daresay she attributed your infirmities to our visit to Spain. Did she assume you'd gotten yourself injured in battle?"

"Good lord, you two think diabolically alike!" He shook his head ruefully. "You mother was not the least concerned over my suffering."

"That was very uncivil of her."

"All of her concern was for my poor mother," he said through gritted teeth.

"And not for this Mrs. Dryden? I've worried myself senseless over you."

He fell back into his pillows and stared at the ceiling.

"Oh, my dearest, I am so sorry. I know how beastly awful you feel. I should never have left you today. I did not like you being alone."

"And I did not like you traipsing around Cotton Lane without me to protect you."

"You're hardly in a position to do much protecting. I am certain Jenkins and Pennington could have protected me and Mrs. Hale most ably."

"I take it Jenkins and Pennington are servants at Sidworth House?"

She nodded.

"Did you find anything at Prufoy's?"

"Not a thing. I did, though, interview a person who actually saw the man who broke into Mr. Prufoy's lodgings."

"Excellent."

She got to her feet. "We'll discuss our investigation as soon as I come back from checking on Annie."

"Apparently your mother gave her some money and sent her off to the green grocer's and to Billingsgate to procure food, which I daresay was a very good thing, and then the woman came back and started cooking."

"Are you hungry?"

"I could eat an elephant."

Picturing her big, strapping husband eating an elephant, she giggled as she left the bedchamber. In the kitchen she found Annie happily stirring pots and chopping vegetables. Annie had come to Sidworth House when she was fourteen. That must have been two or three years earlier, and in those years, she had grown several inches taller. Cook, who became very fond of the fair and frail girl, attributed Annie's growth to her own good cooking.

"Oh, my lady," Annie said, turning as Daphne entered the kitchen, "I am ever so grateful to you for allowing me to become your cook."

Smiling, Daphne ran her eye over the girl. The white apron Annie wore must have been clean that morning, but it was now splotched with green and brown. Despite that her hair had been swept back into a bun, perspiration still beaded on her lightly freckled brow. "Not nearly as grateful as I am to have you. I do hope it won't be too difficult for you to run the kitchen without any help, but you'll just be cooking for the two of us. I think you'll manage beautifully."

Daphne approached the large hearth and peered into the pot. She could not really tell what was cooking, owing to the bubbling and to the fact she knew as much about cooking as she knew about fencing. Which was nothing. "Everything smells delicious. How soon before you can have a meal ready? My husband's famished." How wonderful that sounded! *My husband*.

"In 'alf an hour."

"I beg that you bring our food up to the room at the end of the corridor on the third floor." Daphne started for the door, then turned back. "Have you found your new bedchamber?"

Annie nodded. "Her ladyship told me I could take me pick of the basement rooms."

"I shall have to be very grateful to my mother, then. Please, if you need anything, don't hesitate to ask me."

"Aye, my lady."

* * *

When Daphne returned to Jack's bedchamber, she took a seat in a chair facing him. "Now what do you wish to know?"

She had not noticed he had managed to sit up in bed with his back to the headboard. He would have been incapable of such movement that morning. When he'd said he would be on his feet in three day's time, he hadn't really believed it. Now he was encouraged.

His wife had divested herself of the pelisse and wore a dress of thin cotton embroidered with tiny flowers. He lazily perused her from her bushy locks past her spectacles and down her slender body. She was much to his liking, but he was well aware that he'd found her appearance wanting—until he had fallen irrevocably in love with her.

Could Sir Ronald also be attracted to her? She did not seem his type at all. Sir Ronald's wife, Virginia, was an acknowledged beauty. And quite the opposite of her elder sister, Virginia was possessed of a large bosom.

His gaze fell on Daphne's chest. In today's dress, her breasts filled out the bodice only slightly better than a twelve-year-old lad, but he could not purge from his memory the sweet swell of her breasts beneath the fine lace she'd worn to bed two nights earlier.

How he lamented the fatigue that had robbed him of the enjoyment of making love with his wife that night.

"The description of the murderer?" he finally said.

"Well, I don't exactly have that."

"What *exactly* do you have?"

"He was blond."

"That's all?"

"It was dark. And . . ."

"And what?"

"And my witness is only five years of age."

"Bloody hell!"

She proceeded to tell him what she had learned from the lads and Mrs. Hale.

"Now we must discuss the two lords. Lambeth and Braithwite." He had thought of nothing else all day.

"So do you have any theories?" she asked.

"Possibly."

"Though I am not acquainted with him, I know what Lord Lambeth looks like."

He perked up. "And you're telling me this because. . .?"

"Because he happens to be blond."

"That sounds most promising."

"After what the widow told us about her husband and Lord Lambeth at gaming hells, we shall need to determine if Lord Lambeth had heavy gaming losses."

"And if he's recently come into money."

She bestowed a brilliant smile upon him. "Now, let's move on to Lord Braithwite."

"Wait! How do you propose we investigate Lambeth?" While most women were incapable of analyzing situations, it wasn't like his wife to slip in such a manner.

"Oh, we'll think of something. Let us discuss Lord Braithwite now."

She acted as if she wanted to dismiss Lambeth, which was bizarre, given that she had already insisted she was not acquainted with the man. Why in the hell was she wishing to protect him? "Do you not think it likely Lord Lambeth murdered Prufoy?" he asked.

"Oh, I think it's most probable."

He did too. "So he murdered Prufoy, went to his victim's lodgings, and stole the letters as well as the list."

"Oh, he didn't soil his own hands killing poor Mr. Prufoy."

Jack nodded. "A man's life is cheap to a certain type of man. Offer the wretches a couple of quid and they'd kill their own gin-soaked mothers."

"How I wish I could have paid the vile creatures *not* to kill the dear batman." Her eyes shimmered with unspilt tears. She drew a deep breath. "So after the evil Lord Lambert had Eli Prufoy slain, he proceeded to blackmail my sister and get hordes of money."

"It would seem so."

"So there you have it! Now, what is your opinion regarding Lord Braithwite?"

"I do have an opinion, but it's only a guess."

She leaned toward him, and her spectacles slipped down her nose. "Which is?"

"What if Braithwite's name was on Heffington's list? Neither Prufoy nor Lambeth would have any way of knowing what the list was. Prufoy might have seen Braithwite's name on the list, recognized his importance, and that was the highest-ranking official the major was to deliver the list to."

"What if. . ." She stopped, obviously gathering her thoughts. "What if Lord Lambeth approached

Braithwite and apprised him that he was in possession of a list with his name on it?"

Their eyes locked.

They were both obviously on the same page.

"I believe Lord *Traitorwite* immediately alerted his superior, the vile duc d'Arblier. Of course the duc's first order of business would be to eradicate his number one obstacle, which is you."

"I don't know that I'm that important, but I had reached the same conclusion as you." He was relieved that his wife *was* still possessed of an analytical mind, after all. Independent of him, she had come up with the same theory he had. Only his supposition had taken all day.

"What do you think we should do next?"

"We need to get the list from Lord Lambeth before d'Arblier does. Unfortunately, we must wait until I am more physically capable. The problem is I'm afraid Lambeth will be murdered."

"That's assuming Lambeth is the one with the list—which we're not certain of."

"We need some kind of proof that demonstrates Lambeth has gone from empty pockets to flush purse."

"I shall have to see how Cornelia can assist us in that. If her major had been great friends with Lord Lambeth, she will know all about him. Apparently her flirtation with the major was of some long standing. Truth be told, she's awfully broken up over Major Styles' death."

His eyes narrowed. "It serves her right—not his death, but her remorse."

"I know, my dearest, adultery is extraordinarily disgusting."

Why in the hell was she secretly meeting with that damned baronet?

Their cook entered the chamber, carrying a heavy silver tray laden with tasty-looking food. She was little more than a child.

Daphne hopped up and took the tray, thanking the cook profusely. "It smells lovely. And leek soup is my favorite! Oh, and you've prepared salmon, giblet pie, tongue with redcurrant sauce, peas, and, oh look, Jack, vegetable pudding! I must tell you my husband adores vegetable pudding."

Annie dipped a curtsey as she left the chamber. Daphne brought his plate, but when he went to take it, she shook her head. "Don't you think, dearest, moving your arms, lifting the fork back and forth, will aggravate your wounds?"

"Every movement hurts."

She settled herself on the edge of his bed. "That's why I'm going to feed you."

"Now see here, Daphne! I am not a child."

Her eyes raked over his body. She swallowed and gave him a most somber gaze. "I am well aware of that, Captain. You're the most masculine man I know."

The seductiveness of her words made him wish like hell he was not in such bad shape. But as out of charity as he was with his lying wife right now, he would not have made love to her if he'd been in prime condition. "Very well. Just this first day. I will be better tomorrow."

Damn, but the food was awful, but he was so hungry he wouldn't let a little matter like food tasting like old boots deter him from eating. He wondered if his infirmity had affected his sense of taste. Before commenting on it, he waited to see what Daphne's reaction to the food would be.

Once she finished feeding him, she scooted up to his desk to eat her dinner. "I adore leek soup," she said as she plunged her spoon into it. After that first taste, her brows, too, plunged. She quickly rinsed her mouth with claret. "Dearest?"

"Yes?"

"Do you know of a vegetable or legume which most decidedly looks like leeks but most decidedly does not taste like leek?"

He regarded her with amusement. "Perhaps your Annie mistook a hollyhock stalk for leeks."

She shrugged. "I don't believe I will be able to eat this, but I cannot offend the dear girl. How can I be rid of this?"

His gaze dropped to the chamber pot.

She duly dumped her soup into the pottery vessel and replaced its lid. Only the chambermaid need know the mistress disliked Annie's soup. If they had a chambermaid, which they did not seem to have at present.

Next Daphne cut into her giblet pie, then dug in with a spoon. This, too, was followed with lowered brows and a swish of claret. "Dearest?"

He could not repress a smile. "Yes, love?"

"Did you find the giblet pie to be. . . quite the thing?"

"Not quite."

"Then, sir, you must have been enormously hungry to have actually eaten the entire thing!"

"Indeed." He eyed the chamber pot.

She merely nodded, got up from the desk with plate in hand, and slung all the dinner offerings into the crocked receptacle.

"So, my dear, what are you going to do about our incompetent cook?"

"I cannot worry about that now. My husband's been gravely injured, and we must discover the identity of traitors who threaten our kingdom."

A moment later Annie came to collect the plates. Her face brightened when she saw that each bowl and plate had been cleaned. "I remembered, my lady, Cook sayin' as how much Lady Daphne favored leek soup, so I made a big pot. It should last all week."

"How kind of you," Daphne said.

Even though he knew the problem of a cook who could not cook needed to be addressed, he was proud of Daphne's kindness to her young servant.

After Annie gathered up the dinner tray and left, Daphne came to stand beside his bed, stroking his brow as she murmured. "Now that you've had some nourishment, you will need sleep. I thought I'd lie beside you in case you need anything during the night."

How in the hell was he going to be able to sleep with her lying next to him, every intake of her breath an aphrodisiac to him?

$\mathcal{C}$hapter 13

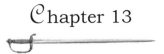

She would not wear her lace night shift until Jack was mended. All that mattered to her now was that he get back on his feet.

In her bedchamber, Daphne donned a cotton cambric night shift with long sleeves, ran a brush through her unmanageable hair, dabbed spear mint behind her ears, then returned to Jack's chamber.

"It's beastly cold in here," she said. "I shall build a fire."

Still propped against the headboard, he regarded her skeptically. "Have you ever built one before?" For the first time all day, there was a bit of a humorous countenance on his (much beloved) face.

"I haven't actually done so, but I've watched the servants build thousands of fires. How difficult could it be?"

Fifteen minutes later, she was almost reduced to tears of frustration. "It looks so easy when others are doing it."

He threw off the covers, but not without grimacing in pain. "I'll do it."

She whirled at him. "You will do no such thing! Perhaps tomorrow you can start using your arms, but I absolutely forbid you to do so tonight."

"I thought you were not going to be a domineering wife," he growled as he swung his legs over the side of the bed.

"Is it being domineering to care about one's husband's wellbeing?"

"I'll not be dictated to."

He limped over to the fire.

She rushed to scoot his wooden desk chair in front of the fire. "Please, dearest, sit. I'm afraid if you squat down, neither of us will be able to get you back up."

He grumbled something she could not understand, then lowered himself into the chair.

She watched in wonder, her mouth gaping open, as he lit the fire in no more than twenty seconds. "That's exactly what I was doing! Why could I not succeed?"

He shrugged. And winced. "I daresay you just need more practice."

"Which I will certainly get if we don't get servants soon."

"Oh, I forgot to tell you. You mother said she's sending over prospective servants for you to interview tomorrow afternoon."

She could tell from the winded way in which he spoke that his simple actions had taxed his lungs. "Allow me to help you back to the bed, dearest."

"I won't have you treating me like I'm a half-wit child."

Nevertheless, she was not about to leave his side. He was so utterly weak.

He went to get up from the chair, and fell back.

"Please, lean on me, just until you're upright."

His next try succeeded. She fastened her arm around him, and together they moved to the bed.

This time he did not attempt to sit. Groaning at the effort, he stretched himself out upon the linen sheets, exhausted. She covered him, then bent to kiss him. Though she intended to kiss his lips, he turned his face away, and she settled for pressing her lips to his cheekbone.

Why did he not want to kiss her? Why in the blazes was he being so beastly curt with her? Not once today had he spoken to her in the soft way he normally did. He acted as if he were angry with her.

Or worse. He acted as if he was no longer in love with her. She circled the foot of the bed and came to lie on the other side, next to her husband. "Should you like me to draw the curtains around the bed?"

"No. I'd just as lief like to see the fire."

"And gloat over your domination over coal, no doubt." Normally, such a comment would elicit a chuckle, but not tonight. Why was he being so cold to her?

She blew out the candle and climbed into his bed. On her belly, she scooted closer to him, then propped herself upon her elbows. "After a good night's rest, you'll be a great deal better." She wanted to touch him but was afraid to hurt him since no part of his face or body had been spared from his attackers. "If you need anything during the night, you must awaken me."

"I'm not going to wake you up," he barked.

She wanted to protest, then she remembered his comment about her being domineering. Nothing could alienate a strong-willed man like Jack more than a domineering wife. How difficult it was for her to be meek and compliant. "I wouldn't mind, love. If the tables were turned, you would assist me, would you not?"

"Of course I would."

"That's what marriage is. We're to be each other's helpmates."

"And always honest with one another, right?"

"Of course."

Soon Jack was sleeping soundly, but sleep eluded her. For hours she lay there in the dark room, listening to Jack's steady breathing, feeling his heat, and asking herself why he was angry with her.

It must just be that he was upset at being injured, upset at the world because of his condition. It wasn't just her he'd been so brusque with. He'd spoken wretchedly about poor, dear Ronnie.

Her thoughts, too, would blend into the investigation they were conducting. Would Ronnie have gone to his clubs tonight? What would she do the following day? The afternoon would be taken up with interviewing prospective servants.

Hopefully another day of rest would help ease Jack back to normalcy. She lay in the darkness and prayed her thanks that Jack's life had been spared. At this time the previous night, she had been mad with worry. With each passing second she had feared she would receive the news that Jack had been murdered.

Even after Sir Ronald had brought her husband's mangled body home, she had been terrified his injuries would prove fatal. When the surgeon assured her he would recover, she had thrown her arms around the neck of the surprised man and thanked him repeatedly.

She finally convinced herself that Jack would be his old cheerful self in the morning.

* * *

Annie awakened them the following morning with a breakfast tray which included a pot of hot coffee. "Just set the tray on the desk," Daphne instructed. "How good of you to bring the food to us, considering my husband's lack of mobility." Daphne left the bed and poured Jack a cup of coffee, added cream and sugar, and took it to him. "Tell me, Annie, how was your room?"

"It was very comfortable, my lady."

"Please let me know if you need anything."

"Oh, I will, my lady."

"Hopefully, you'll soon have company in the servants' quarters. This afternoon I will interview candidates for housekeeper and man servant."

"Very good, my lady." She pulled a letter from her pocket. "This came for you a few minutes ago."

Daphne recognized Sir Ronald's handwriting. How would she explain the letter to Jack? There was nothing for it. She would have to tell a little white lie. It really was for the best. She set it on the desk. "What do you like on your toast, dearest? Black currant or marmalade?"

"Both."

She cut his toast, slathered on both black currant and marmalade, and took Jack his bed tray. "How did you sleep, my dearest?"

"Fine. As long as I didn't have to move." Very slowly, he brought himself into an upright position.

"How are you feeling this morning?"

"Better than yesterday." He bit into the toast.

"That is good news, indeed. I believe you're moving better. I see you're lifting the fork without getting winded."

Nodding solemnly, he eyed her, his gaze still icy. "Why have you not opened your letter?"

She shrugged. "It's just from my sister. I shall read it once you're situated. Is there anything else I can get for you?"

"A new set of ribs?"

"Then they still hurt dreadfully?"

There was resolution in his voice when he said, "I will be better tomorrow."

She sat before his desk and began to pick at her own breakfast, which was most dreadful. She had almost spat out her coffee it was so bad. Were she and Jack going to be saddled with this most dear, inept cook for the rest of their lives? She hadn't the heart to let the poor girl know they were dissatisfied.

Daphne absently broke the seal of Sir Ronald's letter, unfolded it, and read the short missive.

Come to my office at noon to discuss what I've learned.

Sir Ronald

She refolded the letter and glanced at the mantel clock. It was already past ten. She would need to hurry if she wished to be cleaned, dressed, and at Whitehall in an hour and half.

"Well?" Jack asked, glaring her.

"Well what?"

"Are you not going to tell me about the letter you just read?"

"Of course. I will need to meet with Cornelia at noon today."

"Why can't she come here?"

Daphne shrugged. "Because she's a duchess. She's used to having everyone at her beck and call." How she hated lying to her husband. But it was really for his own good. The last thing she wanted was for him to feel inadequate because of his non-aristocratic origins. It was such an easy matter for Sir Ronald to handle this small aspect of their inquiry. "Oh, dear, are you afraid of being left alone again?"

"Madam, there is very little that I'm afraid of."

She knew he feared the duc d'Arblier because the man was so devious. And so evil. It was difficult to fight an unseen enemy, and for d'Arblier, stealth was his most formidable weapon. "Just say the word if you don't want me to leave, and I will stay with you."

He shrugged. "It matters not if you go."

That iciness again! Did she no longer matter to him?

* * *

This was only the second time Daphne had visited Sir Ronald at the Foreign Office, and she nearly blushed remembering the last time when she had come there to steal his seal. But, of course, he had no way of knowing about that. At least, she hoped he did not.

She sat meekly in front of his leather-topped desk, her hands folded in her lap, as he finished giving instructions to the young gentleman who was his secretary. As soon as that gentleman left the chamber, closing the door behind him, Sir Ronald faced her. "How is your husband today?"

"He's better, but still not ambulatory."

"It must be very difficult for an active man like him to lie in bed."

"It's turning him into a positive ogre."

"You'll find marriage isn't always a bed of roses. You must take the good with the bad. Of course, in my marriage," he said, laughing, "it's poor Virginia who has to put up with all the bad."

"My sister would argue that point with you. She adores being your wife."

"I am the most fortunate of men." His brows lowered. "Now as to the situation you asked me to look into. . .I may be too hasty, but Lord Lambeth's sudden ability to pay off all his debts as well as his renewed high stakes play leave little doubt in my mind that Lambeth is the blackmailer."

"And murderer. It does sound as if he's our man!" She told him that Lord Lambeth had bumped into the major's murdered batman when both men called on Mrs. Styles.

"Well, I say, we've all done a bang-up job of sorting all this out."

Instead of gloating, though, over the revelation, she thought of the noble Eli Prufoy, who had been murdered by the greedy Lord Lambeth. Blackmail she almost could have forgiven. After all, Cornelia was no saint. But what of poor Fanny Hale? All she had now of the man she loved was his regimental pin. It was heart breaking. "Do you know if Lord Lambeth is married? I suppose I could I have looked it up in Papa's *Debrett's*."

"He was married some time ago, but his wife died. She was only about five and twenty."

"I daresay she's better off where she is than with him. The vile, contemptuous man."

"Why did you want to know if he's married?"

"Because I need to get into his house. And Cornelia is going to help in that matter." Her gaze fell to the ink well upon his desk. "May I use your pen and paper?"

"Of course."

She quickly penned a note to the duchess. "Could I impose on you yet again?"

"I would be happy to oblige you in any matter, my lady."

She stood and handed the folded missive to him. "Would you see that this is delivered to Lankersham House?"

"I will be happy to. Tell me, my lady, is my dear wife still to remain ignorant of this business?"

"I promised Cornelia. She doesn't like your virtuous wife lecturing her about her lack of morals."

Standing, he chuckled. "May I call a hackney coach for you?"

"Not today. I have our carriage."

His brows lowered. "Your father's?"

"No. The one Jack and I hired to bring us from Portsmouth. We decided to keep if for a few additional days. I couldn't use it the other day because Jack was."

He bowed. "Please let me know if I can be of further assistance."

"You've been wonderfully helpful. I never dreamed you'd make the round of your clubs last night after spending the previous night assisting me and Jack. You must have been exhausted."

"I learned everything I needed to know just by dining at White's. I was home in bed by eleven."

***

Andy was grinning like a newly knighted commoner as she returned to the coach. She hated to think that soon they would have to send him—and the coach—back to Portsmouth. How she would miss them both.

"So this is Whitehall, the seat of British government," he said.

"You're certainly knowledgeable for one so young—and especially for one from the provinces."

"I makes it my business to constantly acquire knowledge, and I can put two and two together—if you know what I mean."

"You're good at mathematics?" she teased.

He opened her carriage door. "I'm good at deducing that you and the captain are involved in clandestine work for his majesty's government."

The sagacity of his comment broadsided her. "If you're as good in mathematics as you are in deduction, you must have been a remarkable student."

His face went somber. "I believe I can be of valuable assistance to you and the captain."

"I believe you will, my dear boy, and I shall apprise my husband of your abilities."

* * *

Daphne barely made it home to Dryden House in time to interview the first candidate for housekeeper, a Mrs. MacInnes, whom Annie had shown to the morning room. The woman had stood and introduced herself when Daphne entered the chamber. Mrs. MacGinnes looked to be well past forty—older than Daphne would have liked. Since they were just starting what Daphne hoped to be a long, happy married life, she had thought she and Jack would surround themselves with a staff that would serve them into old age.

"How very good of you to come," Daphne told her. "Forgive me for just a moment while I look in on my husband. He's recovering from a rather nasty injury." How she loved to refer to Jack as *my husband*! She scurried from the room and raced up two flights of stairs. She couldn't have a moment's peace until she assured herself he had met no harm during her absence. Knowing d'Arblier must be in London worried her more than she would ever allow Jack to know.

She had supplied Jack with pen, paper, and a portable desk top upon which to write in bed while she was gone, and he was scribbling away madly when she threw open his bedchamber door. "Do tell your family we have plenty of room for them when they come to visit us in London, my darling."

He looked up at her, no mirth on his handsome face.

Had her didactic ways angered him? What had gotten into her sweet Jack? Was this the same loving man who had hovered over his heaving wife during the wretched sea voyage? "Forgive me for telling you what to write."

"What did your sister want?"

Oh, dear. She had quite forgotten she had lied about meeting with Cornelia. She shrugged. "You know Cornelia. She thinks the entire world should move at her behest. She thought we should have found out the blackmailer's identity already because she wanted it to be so. We were not able to talk for long because Virginia came—which silenced any further talk of blackmailers. I did have to hurry home to interview our prospective staff—and to check on you." She approached the bed and was powerless to stop herself from dropping a kiss upon his brow.

He stiffened.

And it fairly broke her heart. Her voice softened. "How are you feeling?"

"Not great, but I'll manage."

"You must ring if you need anything, and I must return to a most sour-looking Mrs. MacInnes, who wishes to be our housekeeper."

As she entered the morning room, it occurred to Daphne she knew very little about a housekeeper's duties and even less about interviewing a housekeeper. A pity she hadn't thought to ask her mother for guidance. She took a seat in a faded rose wingback chair facing Mrs. MacInnes. The woman was quite short and quite round. Her black eyes were much the color of Jack's, and Daphne suspected when she was younger, her hair would have been dark like his, but now it was predominately gray—as was her plainly cut dress that was impeccably clean.

"You understand I've just married, and my husband and I are setting up our first home," Daphne began.

"Then this is your first marriage?"

What an audacious woman! Daphne did not need to be reminded she was withering upon the shelf when Jack came into her life. "Indeed. I was quite the spinster."

"Oh, my lady, I didn't mean. . ."

Daphne waved off her apology. "I would prefer in my husband's home not to be addressed as my lady. It's my wish to be known as Mrs. Dryden." She truly loved the sound of it. But then she loved everything about Jack, even the smell of him after he'd been riding hard.

"Very well, my. . .Mrs. Dryden. I meant to ask you a question about the girl who let me in. She said she was your cook, but surely she could not be old enough?"

Daphne sighed. "I daresay she isn't." Lowering her voice, Daphne proceeded to tell her Annie's background—and the dilemma she was presenting to the Dryden household. "I don't know what to do. I cannot hurt her feelings, and I cannot have a cook who cannot cook."

"It's very commendable of you giving the girl a chance. My last employer, Mr. Poyntz—who died several weeks ago—was opposed to taking on servants who had no experience. I always fancied being around young people, and I enjoy teaching young girls how to smoothly run a house. But I do understand you're not planning to have a large staff."

Perhaps Mrs. MacInnes was not so audacious, after all. "Since it is just the two of us. . . You said you were housekeeper to Mr. Poyntz? Would that have been George Poyntz?"

"Aye. I was there these past twelve years."

"His late wife was dear friends with my great aunt Harriet. I used to visit there as a child, but I daresay that would have been before your time. The Poyntz home, as you can easily see," Daphne looked around the small morning room, "is a great deal larger than our home. Would you not be disappointed to come to us where you would not have a large staff to command?"

"I will miss the people with whom I worked, but not the mountain of never-ending responsibilities."

"In a large establishment the housekeeper has to see that her staff sees to all their duties. In a small house, you *are* the staff. You will have to perform tasks that may now seem far beneath your level of experience, things like . . . " Daphne thought of things she only recently realized her staff had always done for her. "Like lighting fires and . . . and making beds—things you won't have had to do in years."

Mrs. MacInnes smiled. "I shan't mind it. Later, after the children come, I daresay you'll need a larger staff."

After the children come. What a lovely thought! "I must tell you we have a chambermaid, but not at present. She's been called away to what may be her mother's death bed."

Mrs. MacGinnes' eyes narrowed in sympathy. "The poor dear."

"If you don't object to starting with virtually nothing, I believe I shall engage you, Mrs. MacInnes."

"Since it appears your need is dire, I would be willing to start immediately."

"You are a jewel!"

"I shall just collect my things and be ready to pitch in wherever I'm needed."

"Good." Daphne rose. "I was to conduct more interviews this afternoon, but I have many other pressing matters to attend. Would it bother you terribly if we do not procure a man servant right away?"

Mrs. MacInnes rose. The top of her head was level with Daphne's chin. "Give me a ladder, and I can handle anything a man can!"

"Excellent!" Daphne was happy to acknowledge her own mistaken first impression of Mrs. MacInnes.

"And. . ." the new housekeeper lowered her voice. "Just leave your problem with the young cook to me. I learned a thing or two about cooking at my mother's knee."

"You are wonderful!"

There was a rap at the front door.

"Should you like me to get the door, Mrs. Dryden?"

"Yes, thank you." Daphne was very pleased with herself. She now believed Mrs. MacInnes was just the person to manage their home.

The new housekeeper showed Cornelia into the morning room, and as Daphne faced her, she put her index finger to her lips and whispered. "I don't want Jack to know you're here."

"Why, pray tell?"

"Because I told him a haughty duchess expected others to come to her—and he believes I've already been to see you today."

Scowling at her sister, Cornelia plopped onto the faded brocade sofa. "Lying to one's husband is no way to start a marriage."

Daphne rolled her eyes heavenward. "Quoteth Isabelle de Merteiul to Hannah More."

"I did not know my Hannah More-admiring sister had actually read *Les Liaison dangereuses*."

"I'm the sister who's always reading, and I have the deficient vision to show for it. But we must hurry and get to the point."

"Which is? Why have you summoned me here? I'll have you know I had many important things to see to this afternoon."

Daphne thrust hands to hips and glared at her sister. "Do you have any idea at all what my husband and I have gone through to get those wretched letters back for you?"

"Oh, I am dreadfully sorry, Daf. I truly am utterly grateful to you and Cap--- what is this

Virginia was telling me about Sir Ronald saving your captain's life?"

"Virginia would see Sir Ronald as the hero." Daphne frowned. "I will admit he was wonderfully helpful. I had to call him when Jack did not return from visiting Major Styles' widow."

Cornelia's brows hiked.

"He was followed—and attacked."

"Oh, how horrid! That Styles woman must be responsible!"

"I don't think she was behind it at all. She's a perfectly nice woman." Daphne lowered her voice. "Jack's in bed upstairs now, assuring me that he will be back to walking in two more days."

"He cannot walk?"

"Well, he can hobble, but it's still quite painful, but that's enough talk of Jack now. I asked you here because I believe we have learned who has the letters."

"Who?"

"Lord Lambeth. I'm assuming you know him?"

The duchess's eyes widened. "Indeed. He and Major Styles were very close friends. They'd been at Harrow together."

"Apparently, they were so close that he knew you had written romantic letters to the major. I believe he may have murdered Major Styles' batman in order to take possession of the letters."

"What a detestable, contemptible, vile, odious, wicked, wicked man! And to think, he always treated me with such great admiration. How could the fiend do this to me?" She clutched at her chest with a great dramatic flair.

"He did much worse to the poor batman!"

"There is that. Added to Lambert's other disgusting offenses, he's a sinister murderer." Her eyes narrowed as she looked at Daphne. "What do we do now?"

"Jack and I need to search his house. I'm hoping Jack will be up to it tomorrow night. I will be counting on you to insure that Lord Lambeth's not at home. Do whatever it takes to have him come to you tomorrow night."

Cornelia's eyes widened. "But the man's a murderer!"

"He's not going to kill you. If he's always treated you with admiration, he will likely hope to start a *flirtation* with you. Promise him a flirtation. You only have to see him for one night."

Cornelia gave a bitter laugh. "That shouldn't be difficult. He's always had designs on me. Though I daresay I don't know how I could possibly be civil to the vile, disgusting, larcenous, murdering swine."

In this, the two sisters were in perfect agreement.

After she saw her sister to the door, Daphne began to mount the stairs. She drew in a deep breath. Now she would have to tell more lies to her husband.

$\mathcal{C}$hapter 14

"Oh, my dearest, we've been positively brilliant!" She eyed her handsome husband sitting in the big bed glaring at her. The purple around his eye socket was turning black and his swelling had gone down, but the cut on his lips did not appear to be healing. He did emanate a strength that had been absent the day before. And it was not just because of his massive shoulders and long trunk—attributes no prospective murderers could diminish.

"Brilliant?"

"I know. I know," she defended. "You do not want me to use that word in connection with you."

He was still out of charity with her, and she wished like the devil she knew why. "Cornelia has just been here, and she has virtual proof that all of our deductions have been correct."

His brows lowered above shimmering obsidian eyes. "About Lambeth?"

"Indeed." She came to sit on the side of his bed and stroke the smooth planes of his tanned face. "You're looking much better. Your voice is stronger, and look at you! You're sitting up, looking your old supremely masculine self."

"Supremely?" He glowered.

She shrugged. "I cannot help speaking my mind. It is, after all, just the two of us, and we are man and wife."

"You, madam, are incorrigible, but you are correct about the state of my health. I do feel much more the thing."

"That is very good since we have a mission to accomplish tomorrow night."

"Whoa! Back up. What has the duchess confirmed?"

"While we cannot know that with certainty, it seems obvious that Lambeth is the blackmailer."

"And why does it seem so obvious?"

"Because mere weeks ago the viscount was deeply in debt, and now he's positively oozing funds, paying off all his debts and engaging once more in high-stakes play."

"And you know this because?"

"Cornelia has just confirmed everything." Daphne hated lying to her husband but consoled herself with the knowledge that everything she was telling him was true—except for the source of her knowledge regarding Lord Lambeth. "First, she confirmed that Lord Lambeth and Major Styles were extremely close friends. They were at Harrow together."

He nodded. "So it's likely Lambeth knew about the relationship between his friend and your sister."

"And he probably knew, too, that she'd written him letters. A husband who would be unfaithful to such a lovely woman as Mrs. Styles would be just the sort to brag to his friend about a duchess writing him love letters."

Jack nodded in agreement. "What else did the duchess confirm?"

"The duke was witness to Lambeth engaging in very deep play at faro the past several nights at White's—after settling all his debts." Daphne made a silent vow that when all of this was over, she would never again lie to her husband.

"And now, madam, explain this mission of ours."

While she adored being Mrs. Dryden, she did not adore being referred to as madam. Coming from Jack's lips, there was a certain hostility to it. Perhaps her authoritarian ways were a threat to his masculinity. Perhaps she should allow him to determine the next step. "That is really for you to decide. After all, you're the expert at espionage. Or is *expert* one of those words you do not like me attaching to you?"

He started to laugh.

It was like blue skies after days of relentless rains. She smiled back. "What I am trying to convey," she said, "is that you should plan our next step. You have so much more experience than me at such matters. How do you propose we get the papers from Lambeth?"

"We steal them."

Exactly what she planned, but of course, she would let him take credit for their mission. "Do you think you'll be up to it tomorrow night?"

"I will."

She could not help herself. She threw her arms around him. When she went to kiss him, it pleased her that he settled soft lips over hers, groaned, then enclosed her in his strong embrace.

Before matters could heat up in the way she wished, a knock sounded at her door.

Jack groaned again.

Daphne sat up, ramrod straight. "Come in."

The portly Mrs. MacInnes waddled into the chamber, bearing a letter on a silver tray. "This just came for you, Mrs. Dryden."

"Thank you." Daphne proceeded to introduce the new housekeeper to Jack as she eyed Virginia's seal. After Mrs. MacInnes departed, Daphne opened the letter and quickly read it. "Blast it all!"

"What's wrong?"

"Virginia says Mama needs me this afternoon."

"Then you must go to her."

Her gaze went to his sword, and she brought it to stand up propped against the wall by his bed. "I will feel better knowing you have some protection."

"Why does our new housekeeper call you Mrs. Dryden? Does she not know you're the daughter of an earl and as such should be addressed as Lady Daphne?"

Daphne got to her feet, put hands to sides, and glared at the man she had married. "As much as I love Papa, you're first in my life now. I'm proud to be known as Mrs. Dryden."

His dark eyes sparkling, her husband silently regarded her as she took her leave.

* * *

Daphne had not been gone ten minutes when Virginia called on Jack. Mrs. MacInnes showed her into Jack's chamber. Impotent though he was to do anything about it, he was nevertheless embarrassed for Sir Ronald's wife to see him so jessified. He must project masculinity with his voice. "How good of you to call, Lady Virginia." Had he sounded strident enough?

His gaze locked with hers. She was a remarkably lovely creature. So much like the duchess, but rather taller and statuesque. Her eyes glistened, and she immediately burst into tears.

He went to leap from his bed in order to comfort her, but his wounded body would not oblige. He tried once more and slowly rose. He was grateful his long nightshirt covered what needed to be covered. "Pray, my lady, what is the matter?" Should he put an arm around her? Or would that be too intimate since he was standing in his bedchamber wearing a nightshirt? She was, after all, another man's wife.

And he was another woman's husband.

His gallantry extended to merely handing the weeping woman his handkerchief.

"Your wife is secretly seeing my husband."

Good God, he felt as if he'd been knifed in the gut. This hysterical woman was confirming his worst suspicions. He drew in a deep breath. "I cannot allow you to malign my wife in such a manner."

She sank into an upholstered chair. "Why would Daphne do this to me?"

"Why would you impugn her in this manner? Daphne is loyal to those she loves. And that includes me." He recalled Daphne's last words to him that afternoon. He was most important to her. No matter how things looked—and he admitted they looked rather woeful—he had faith in his wife.

"But I saw them with my own eyes! Not once but twice!"

He had seen them, too. But there had to be another explanation. "Please, my lady, calm yourself and explain."

She took a deep sniff, dried her tears, and faced him. The same haunting look he'd seen on Mrs. Styles' face was mirrored in Virginia's pretty face. "I confess I did not see them together the first time when they met in a hackney carriage, but the man I hired to follow my husband did."

What kind of obsessed woman would actually hire someone to spy on her husband? "Pray, my lady, why did you hire a man to shadow Sir Ronald?"

She did not answer for a moment. "I need to know I am the only woman in his life."

"How do you know you can trust this man you hired?"

"He came most highly recommended."

"I assure you, if Sir Ronald met with my wife, it was completely innocent. Perhaps they are planning a surprise for you. Do you have a birthday coming up? Or a special occasion?" God, he hoped so.

She shook her head morosely, tears gathering once again.

That walloping feeling in his gut returned. "And the second time?"

"Noon today. She met him in his office."

His face fell. *She's lied to me again.* "I may not know a great deal about conducting affairs, but I'm reasonably sure they are not conducted in the middle of the day at the Foreign Office. "

She thought on this for a moment, then brightened. "I will give you that."

"Now, about that first clandestine meeting. . .did your man see the hackney take the accused lovers to a bagnio or some such location where adulterous . . . activities take place?" He knew very well they did not.

"Not actually."

"Do you mean they just drove around in the hackney with curtains drawn, conducting their illicit affair within?" He knew very well that had not occurred, either.

"Well, not actually."

"Tell me, then, what did occur?"

"Daphne arrived at the Foreign Office in a hackney coach and summoned my husband. He came to the coach, got in, and they . . . they stayed within for a few minutes, then Ronnie returned to his post."

"You must admit, my lady, all of this sounds rather innocent." God, he hoped it was. But what in the hell could it be? And why in the hell was Daphne lying to him?

"I needed to see you today, to see if you really were injured. That's how Ronnie explained his absence two nights ago."

He held out his arms. "See for yourself how pitiable I am, my lady. Your husband did, indeed, haul my mangled body home to restore me to my worried wife that night. Three men apparently wished me dead." Jack sat on the side of his bed. "Forgive me for my state of undress."

"I'm dreadfully sorry, Captain. For everything. About Ronnie. . .one more thing. Last night, he said he was at White's."

"I assure you, Daphne was with me the whole evening." *White's?* Isn't that where Daphne said the Duke of Lankersham had seen Lord Lambeth gambling? Had she substituted the duke's name for Sir Ronald's? Why would she do something so pointlessly dishonest? This really was out of character for Daphne, who was inherently a most honest woman.

Virginia stood. "Since I needed to speak to you alone, I concocted a story to get her to my parents' house. I'd best be back before Daphne returns because she's apt to be angry with me."

She went to the door, then turned back. "I shouldn't have barged in on you—in your condition, but I must say you've eased my worried mind enormously."

* * *

"Daphne! How good it is to see you! Allow me to look at you." Lady Sidworth proceeded to rise from the little French desk in her study where she had been scribbling letters, then she circled her eldest daughter. "The captain assured me you were not injured in Spain by those wretched French murderers who nearly killed him." She shook her head. "I don't know how his mother can bear it."

Daphne's mouth dropped open to protest, but her mother raced on.

"Your husband tells me you were dreadfully sick during the crossing. I daresay you took that from your papa. I shall never forget our wedding trip aboard the Sidworth yacht—which you will not remember---"

"Of course I couldn't remember your wedding trip since I wasn't yet born."

Lady Sidworth vigorously shook her head. "What I was going to say was you won't remember the yacht because Sidworth sold it immediately after the wedding trip and said he would never again step foot aboard a bloody boat—pardon my language, but your father introduced me to the most vile language imaginable during our wedding trip, most of it as he retched into the unmentionable, unmentionable, unmentionable basin." She shook her head. "It was not a happy wedding trip."

"Nor was mine." Daphne dropped onto a pale yellow damask settee, and her mother came to sit next to her. "But other than the sea voyage, our wedding trip has been particularly wonderful." Except for that one matter.

"How is Annie working out?"

She did not answer for a moment. "She needs a bit more experience." To change the topic and not malign poor Annie, Daphne continued, "And I've engaged the Poyntz's former housekeeper, who seems wonderfully capable."

"I am gratified that all is working out for you. I've been dreadfully worried."

Daphne rose. "You have now seen with your own eyes that I am in perfect good health. Now I really must return to my ailing husband. I do so worry about him." Especially knowing that d'Arblier must be in London planning to assassinate Jack. If he knew of Jack's weakened state, he could be just bold enough to stage an audacious daytime attack.

$\mathcal{C}$hapter 15

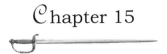

"Are you certain, dearest, that you're physically capable of performing tonight's mission?" Daphne had to admit that in the four and twenty hours since she'd left her mother's house Jack had demonstrated remarkable progress. Even if he was excessively brooding. She supposed his dislike of inactivity accounted for his irritability.

While he had refused to lie in bed, his movements were severely impeded by the soreness in his ribs, a shoulder that would not budge, and swelling around his knee.

They had actually ventured a trip to Lankersham House, and together with Cornelia, planned their clandestine mission. Cornelia had been sending letters back and forth to Lord Lambeth regarding their night's rendezvous.

Daphne then set about copying the viscount's handwriting—something she had a remarkable proficiency for—then drafted a note that would be delivered to the Lambeth servants that evening, purportedly from their master, giving all of them the evening off.

Cornelia's most significant contribution to their mission was her ability to get her hands on the plans for Lord Lambeth's house on Manchester Square, which had been built in the last century by Robert Adam. After memorizing the layout of the house, Jack and Daphne decided upon entering through a window in the library, which was located on the ground floor at the back of the house. They had previously selected the library as the first room to examine. She just hoped Lord Lambeth's taste did not extend to bibliophilic acquisitions since they needed to check every book in the chamber.

Daphne's biggest obstacle in the planning stages was convincing Jack to allow her to come along on the mission. He had been vehemently opposed to putting his wife at risk. She and Cornelia used all their persuasive powers to convince him that Daphne's aid would be most helpful and that no harm could possibly befall her as long as Jack was there to protect her. Daphne knew without a doubt he would lay down his own life to protect hers.

"Of course I am fit enough for our mission!" he snapped.

"I could always have Sir Ronald accompany us. He's not only a noted pugilist---"

"Yes, I know." He spoke through gritted teeth as he rolled his eyes. "I am well aware that Sir Ronald is handy with a sword—even if he's never been in face-to-face combat with an enemy whose object was to kill him."

The very idea of Jack standing face-to-face with a horrid man like the duc d'Arblier gave her a sinking feeling. Her poor Jack. He was low because of his infirmity and, quite naturally, a bit resentful of Sir Ronald's robust good health and many manly strengths. "I daresay you could easily best Sir Ronald if you were not injured."

It was now half past eleven. They had sent around a letter dismissing the Lambeth servants at eight that night.

She donned her full-length black cloak over a black dress. She hadn't worn it since she'd been in mourning for her grandfather. Jack, too, donned a black cloak.

As Andy stood there in the dark, holding open the coach door, Daphne decided to take the lad into her confidence. When she had discussed him with Jack, he had not been adverse to trusting the young coachman. "Pray, Andy, can you be entrusted with a secret?"

"Ye can count on me integrity, my lady." He seemed to have grown two inches taller.

She stifled a laugh and lowered her voice to just above a whisper. "The captain and I are on an important mission for the crown---"

Jack's fingers clamped her arm. "Now, my dearest wife, you mustn't go about attaching such undo importance to this."

"But, darling, Andy will be an important part of our investigation." She directed her attention back to the young coachman. "We hope to expose French spies right here in London." She knew such knowledge would play to the lad's adventurous spirit. And to his patriotism.

Jack's grip became tighter. "Into the coach, madam." He did not sound happy.

A beaming Andy let down the steps. "I am honored to be taken into your confidence, and I'll do me best to assist in any way I'm needed." Andy was so intrinsically likeable she had no reservations about trusting him.

Jack gave their destination to Andy. "And while we are within the premises there, you will need to continue circling the square. It might be necessary---"

"To make a swift get-away?" Andy asked, his face shining with admiration.

Jack sighed.

Before he closed the coach door, Andy quickly calculated the best route to Manchester Square. The lad's memorization of those London maps was proving to be most useful.

"One thing more," Daphne said. "We shall enter the premises through the back."

"Very good, my lady."

During the hours of their preparation, Jack had drummed into Daphne the necessity of precision planning. Every detail—as well as any possible interruption—must be anticipated, every move committed to memory. "A mission's success," he had chanted, "hinges on good planning."

After the coach began to move, Jack turned to her. "My dear wife, do you not realize that spies cannot go around announcing their clandestine activities publicly?"

"Andy is NOT the public. He's a good lad, and by taking him into our confidence we have recruited an invaluable ally."

"In the future, I request that you and I together make such a determination."

"Of course you're right, my love, but you did say you trusted the boy."

"Trusting him and blurting out state secrets to him are two entirely different matters!"

She pouted. "You're not happy with me."

"Is it too much to ask that before you go around recruiting . . . associates, you and I first discuss it?"

"I shall defer to you in the future," she answered, her tone contrite.

Throughout the coach ride to Manchester Square, they continued to go over their plan until Jack finally deemed Daphne adequately prepared.

She lifted the velvet curtain from the window. "We're here. Andy's slowing at the lane to the Lambeth mews." And the back of Lambeth House.

She peered from her window, Jack from his. Andy had been instructed to continue on should there be any persons in the lane. He came to a dead stop.

Jack turned to her. "I really don't like endangering you like this. I wish you would stay in the carriage."

"How little you know me, sir, if you think I could even for a second contemplate allowing my husband to go in there without me."

He muttered an oath and exited the coach, then turned back to assist her. In their dark clothing they sidled along the lane until they came to a stately home of Portland stone, the house Robert Adam had built for Lord Lambeth's father. "This is it," she whispered, not without a trembling inside. What if Lord Lambeth was still within? Or what if she and Jack climbed through that window and met the barrel of a musket?

They both knew the house's layout from memory, both walked to the last window on the ground floor. Its sill met Jack's chin. He stopped and turned back. There was enough of a moon that the features of his face were identifiable. Though he'd been on possibly hundreds of missions, the concern etched upon his face bore the unmistakable signs of worry. Her presence must weigh on him like an unnecessary appendage.

She would just have to prove her worth.

He went to work quickly, and opened the library window with little effort. Then he gave Daphne a leg up. They had decided she would go in first because she was too short to get in without assistance. (She rather liked being thought of as short—since most of her life she had towered over most of her female acquaintances.)

Once she was clear of the window frame and standing within Lord Lambeth's library, she took stock of her surroundings. No sounds. She could see very little, owing to the darkness. Then she turned back to the opened window. Jack was attempting to hoist himself in, but was having a great deal of difficulty because of his badly bruised (and probably broken) ribs and injured shoulder. "Please allow me to drop down a chair for you to stand upon," she whispered.

"I'm not going to stand on a bloody chair." He mumbled something about being jessified as he grimaced and groaned and eventually succeeded in forcing himself up.

Inside the library, Jack lit a candle and handed it to her. Her worth had been reduced to her ability to hold a light for her husband. Now rudimentally illuminated, the chamber featured just five banks of floor-to-ceiling bookcases. Exactly as she had hoped. Most men who were enamored of high-stakes play were *not* bibliophiles. Thank goodness.

Jack started with the shelves that were eye level, taking a single book, shaking it spine up, then tossing it to the floor. He cleaned every book from the shelf.

Just as he was attempting the next shelf, the door to the room began to creak open.

They both stilled. Jack whispered in her ear. "You must go back."

While she was not one to flee a sinking ship—especially when that ship held her husband—she reasoned her best chances of helping both of them from a potential scrape was for her to be free of the house.

She slithered toward the still-open window, terrified when the library door came fully open. Her head swiveled to see the intruder, but it was much too dark for recognition. All she could tell was that it was a man, and he was smaller than Jack—the knowledge of which should give her comfort. But it did not, especially when his footsteps most definitely moved into the chamber they were in.

As she drew next to the open window, she gathered the dark velvet draperies around her, sat on the window sill, spun around, then dropped to the pavement below.

Jack must have taken that opportunity to attack the intruder because the unmistakable sounds of a scuffle brought terror to her heart.

She stood upon her tiptoes to try to peer into the chamber just in time for her face to be the receptacle of a man's boot. The boot's force knocked her to the ground.

A string of French curse words followed, then the intruder leapt to the ground and raced away.

The moon glistened upon the knife in his hand.

$\mathcal{C}$hapter 16

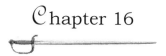

Jack! The knife!

She did not care if they were caught where they ought not to be. All that mattered was Jack. She called his name and realized she sounded like a warbler's death call. If there was such a thing.

In an effort to hoist herself back through the window, she clawed at the Portland stone but was neither tall enough, nor strong enough to succeed. As she stood upon her tiptoes gazing through the open window, she was rewarded with a wondrous sight: Jack.

Though the sight was wondrous, the words spouting from his mouth were not. He was not pleased.

"Thank God you're unhurt," she whispered.

"When I heard your scream, I thought that fiend had hurt you."

"Do you know who that fiend was?"

"Dear God, was it d'Arblier?"

She nodded solemnly. "Possibly. He was definitely French and the same size—and hair color—as the duc."

And those vile words erupted again in a fierce cacophony that concluded with Jack's apology. "Forgive me, but I am not happy. I could have had him if it weren't for my damned shoulder."

"Still unable to move it?"

"Regrettably." As he spoke to her, he had been leaning out the window. Then he straightened, ears perked like one of her papa's pointers. "I do believe there's not a single servant here. Your screech certainly would have alerted one."

Screech? She supposed that wail had come off sounding rather like a screech. If she were a more feminine creature, like Cornelia or Virginia, she would have resented his description. A proper lady did not screech. Thank God she was not a feminine creature. "Then I say why don't we light all the candles and have a good go at the room?"

"A very good suggestion. Here, allow me to help you back in." He reached for her.

She shook her head. "You must have a care for that shoulder. I'll come in the back door, if you unlock it for me."

A moment later they were together back in the library. He found and lighted an oil lamp, which illuminated the small celery-colored chamber of dark woods. The room featured two doors, one to the central hallway and the other to Lord Lambeth's study, which was an even smaller room. "Since we may have rather free rein, shall we peruse his lordship's study? That's where the Frenchman came from" she said.

Not waiting for his reply, she started for the adjacent room.

Jack opened the door. "After you, my lady."

Still holding the oil lamp, she strode into the chamber. Papers were strewn on the floor, and it appeared the drawers of Lord Lambeth's desk had been emptied. She approached the desk. On the floor beneath the desk she saw something that made her drop the lamp and cry out again.

This time it was worse than a screech.

Jack rushed to her side to restore the lamp to an upright position before it burned the carpet. Then he followed her gaze and saw the crumpled, bloody body of a man with blond hair. "Lambeth?"

Tears stinging her eyes, she nodded solemnly.

Jack dropped to his knees—not spryly, but with the agility of an eighty year old—and felt for Lord Lambeth's pulse. Seconds later, he looked up solemnly and shook his head.

She was sickened and felt like bawling, but not for the wicked man who lay dead almost at her feet, the man who had likely murdered the honorable Mr. Prufoy. She knew it had been the duc's knife which had killed the viscount, and she quaked at the thought that it could have been Jack.

Her husband stood, drew her into his embrace, and held her. Soft kisses pressed into her hair, accompanied by low murmurs of assurance. "I am so sorry you had to see this."

She hated to think of all the deaths Jack had witnessed. This was her first. Elderly grandparents laid out on a bier did not count.

Jack's embrace and gentle words banished the sobs which had been on the precipice of erupting. "I am just so very grateful it wasn't you." She looked up into his face and stroked his finely chiseled cheek.

That was when she saw the blood on her hand. Blood from Jack.

"You've been hurt!" Her heartbeat thundered, her hands trembled.

"It was too dark for me to see his knife." Jack shrugged. "I may have gotten a small flesh wound."

That he was standing there communicating with her demonstrated that he had not been badly wounded. But she was incapable of rational thought. Nothing could be more terrifying than the very idea of a knife searing her husband's flesh. (Well, actually seeing such an action would undoubtedly be worse.) She dropped to the floor as if felled by a musket ball and began to sob.

This was not a my-family's-faithful-dog-died sob. It was the kind of sob which might burst forth from a mother who'd just seen her entire family—which included five precious children—slaughtered before her very eyes.

Daphne did not understand how she could have become so hysterical when a (relatively) healthy Jack stood before her.

His brows lowered with concern, he squatted beside her. "There, now. What's the matter, love? I'm not really injured. I barely feel it."

Then he tossed off his cape. This was followed by the removal of his jacket. Next—but not without wincing in pain—he pulled off his shirt. Even streaked with blood, his upper torso was a magnificent sight. Her gaze raked over the rock-hard muscles moistened with perspiration from his recent fisticuffs and a spray of fine black hair in the center of his chest, and her heartbeat galloped.

What in the great, wide world was Jack doing?

"You can see the wound for yourself," he said, his voice low and husky, yet incredibly gentle. "It's not deep." He presented his back to her.

Still incoherent and sobbing and sniffing plentifully, she eyed the gash on his back close to the armpit. It was bleeding dreadfully, but no inner parts seemed in danger of spilling from the site.

Even though she was reassured, her sobs would not subside.

He planted his bottom firmly on the floor and yanked her into his arms. For several minutes he held her tightly. "I've seen this kind of hysteria after battle. It's really not uncommon. You must understand, I'm relatively unhurt. You're unhurt. We apparently stopped d'Arblier from getting his hands on the list. I'd say this has been a successful mission."

His words finally broke through the hysteria. "You really think we stopped the vile man?"

His grip tightened about her for a fraction of a second. "I'm convinced of it. Remember, it was but seconds after I tossed the books to the floor—which, you must admit, I was not very quiet about—he opened that door."

"That's right! We obviously interrupted him. But I don't understand why you had to go and fight with him. Could you not have stood silently in the dark?"

"I've been trained to leave no stone unturned. I couldn't allow someone to get away without trying to determine who it was and if he'd learned anything."

"That was before you married. I shall be very happy when this business is over with. You have no regard for your own neck."

"I most certainly do. It's just that I love England more."

She could have wept anew over how honorable the man she married was. "Allow me to dress your wound."

He nodded ruefully. "The bloody assassin ruined my jacket."

"Better that than you."

"Were I not suffering the effects of my recent attack, I know I could have bested the bast- -" He coughed. "You must forgive my regrettable tongue."

"And you must quit thinking of me as a lady. I'd be ever so appreciative if you'd think of me as one of the bloods."

He ran a seductive gaze down her from the tip of her head to the hem of the cape she still wore, to her exposed ankle. "Impossible." Then he puckered his lips, quickly kissed her, and set her down as he got to his feet. "Allow me to help you up, my lady."

She put her hand into his, and he drew her to a standing position. Her eyes never left the panel of silken draperies that covered the window. "The lining of these will have to do to bind your wound. Do you think you can remove them for me? They're rather high up."

He ended up having to fetch the library steps in order to reach the top of the drapery. After he presented a twelve-foot long panel to her, she set to work tearing the white dimity lining into long strips. Because the sun had made the cloth rather fragile, it tore remarkably easily. "We'll have to clean your wound when we get home," she said. "All we can do now is staunch the bleeding." She proceeded to wind the strips around Jack's upper torso as if he were a mummy.

It was an exceedingly difficult task for her, owing to her propensity to want to be held against his gleaming, taut, statue-worthy chest. By the time she was finished, her breathing had become raspy. She told herself not to think about Jack. *I must concentrate on our mission.* "What do we do now?" she managed to ask.

"We find what d'Arblier was looking for." He put his shirt back on, then the bloodied jacket, but he held off on donning the heavy black cloak—which she thought a very good idea.

She divested herself of the long, black cloak she wore. "You're sure the Frenchman didn't find it?"

"Almost certainly."

Her gaze went back to the dead body. "What do we do with Lord Slimebeth?"

"We shall allow his servants to deal with it tomorrow." His glance went to the clock on the chimneypiece. "Or, I should say, later today." He sombered. "Will it bother you terribly?"

"I am not in the least sorry that that horrid man has received his proper comeuppance. It's just that's it's so beastly mortifying to be in the same room with such a horrifying sight— especially when we, too, were in the same room with his murderer!"

"There is that." Then Jack brightened. "I'll just scoot Lambeth into the corridor so we can set about our search."

As he dragged the dead body to the central hallway, she strolled beside him as if lugging around a dead body were an everyday occurrence. Instead of leaving the corpse there on the polished wooden floor, he began to stuff it into a cupboard of the hall's large Elizabethan sideboard.

"You can't do that by yourself!" she protested, rushing to assist him. Did the foolish man not realize the limitations imposed by his injuries?

She took Lord Lambeth's boots and lifted. "I wonder if these boots would fit our Andy. Did you not notice the holes in the poor boy's soles? And these are so very fine. I daresay the scoundrel purchased them with money wrung from my poor sister."

Her husband scowled. "I draw the line at disrobing dead men."

"You, my dearest love, are such a prude."

Ignoring her, he forced the viscount's stiffened legs into the cabinet and slammed the door shut. "If it's dark, the servants probably won't see the trail of blood."

Jack and Daphne returned to the study.

"Dearest?"

"Yes?"

"Why do you think the duc d'Arblier would have searched the study first instead of the library?"

"Because that is where Lambeth was. D'Arblier must have come here with the intention of killing him. If it was the duc."

"I believe it was the duc, and I believe he must have been here for some time. Wasn't the viscount supposed to have left at nine to meet Cornelia?"

"You know very well he was. You know every calculated move of this mission as well as I." He glared.

She mimicked a man's voice. "The success of a mission hinges on precision planning."

His gaze circled the dimly lit room. "It does appear the duc gave this room a thorough search."

"This was the second chamber we were going to search—if the library did not yield what we were looking for."

Not only had every drawer of the large desk been cleaned out, it also appeared that every single piece of paper must have been examined.

And there were many. Hundreds of sheets of foolscap and parchment nearly covered the room's Turkey carpet.

"If he looked at every single sheet of paper, that could certainly account for why the duc spent two hours here."

Jack nodded. "I'm just wondering if we should re-examine each piece of paper."

She groaned. "Surely not."

"Not now. We'll continue with our plan."

"And if the library fails to yield the precious purloined papers, we come here?"

"Exactly." He snatched up the oil lamp and started for the adjoining chamber.

Now it was she who was mumbling unmentionable words under her breath as she strode back through the connecting door to the library.

No longer consigned to the task of holding a candle, she was now free to search the lower shelves of the bookcases while Jack teetered on library steps in order to reach the upper shelves.

The first three sets of lower shelves proved fruitless, but on the next a folded piece of paper fluttered to the floor when Daphne shook a poetry book.

"I found something!"

Jack turned to watch as she picked up the paper and began to unfold it.

Her heart fell. "It's just a most amateurish effort at love poetry."

He sighed. "Carry on."

Within fifteen minutes they had searched the entire chamber. Every book had been examined. Every sofa pillow was removed, revealing no papers hidden beneath. While Jack searched behind the pictures hanging on the wall, Daphne lay on the floor and peered beneath the room's two sofas, but there was nothing to be found.

With eyes narrowed, she looked at her husband.

"Yes, love. We now search every single paper in the next chamber."

* * *

A few minutes into their examination of the papers, the rear door to the house creaked opened. He stilled. What if d'Arblier had come back—this time with armed men? He should never have allowed Daphne to come.

The footsteps continued on down the stairs to the basement, where the servants' rooms were located.

"I suppose when the servants see the lamp on here, they'll assume it's Lord Blackmailer," Daphne whispered, her nose wrinkled with disdain.

He nodded. "I just hope they don't see the blood."

They both went back to reading snippets of letters that ranged from instructions to Lambeth's steward to bills from tradesmen demanding payment. There were also crude letters written by Lambeth's inamoratas—but no letters written by Cornelia to Major Styles.

"Here's one of Cornelia's notes to Lord Blackmailer about tonight's assignation," Daphne said, her eyes running over the page, her mouth lifted into a smile. *"I've always had a tendre for you. . ."* Daphne shook her head. "It appears my sister is possessed of a talent for writing amorous letters."

"This is one time it has proven harmless."

"You really shouldn't speak ill of Cornelia. Had it not been for her association with Major Styles, we would never have been so successful in our quest. The duc d'Arblier's interest only confirms that all our assumptions have been correct."

"Not assumptions. Hypotheses."

She nodded. "There is rather a distinction between the two, and you, my brilliant husband, are right, of course."

He glowered. "What did I tell you about---"

"I know, I know. I'm not to say you're brilliant. Even if you are."

This time he ignored the incorrigible woman. "Why do you not gather up a pile of paper and come sit closer to the oil lamp?"

He might be the one who was injured, but his wife looked excessively tired. She stacked up a sizeable pile of papers that had been discarded by the Frenchman, moved next to him, and began to read the top paper from her stack. She had to hold it to within mere inches from her spectacles in order to make out the tiny print. Another sure sign of her fatigue.

He should not have subjected her to all she'd had to endure that night.

He shouldn't have listened when she and that philandering sister of hers persuaded him to allow Daphne to join him on this mission. She could have been killed. He still trembled from the fear that had spiked through him when she'd shrieked as d'Arblier brushed past her. For a paralyzing second, he had thought the knife which only grazed him may have plunged into his beloved wife.

His thoughts turned back to the papers he was perusing. The one on top of his stack was a playbill from Haymarket. He tossed it aside. The next was a letter from Lord Marchton that demanded payment of a gambling debt in the amount of twelve hundred guineas. Next came another request for settling a gambling debt, this one from Sir Edward Ferguson for some seven-hundred-forty-three pounds.

Daphne had become suspiciously quiet. He looked up at her and discovered she had fallen asleep sitting up. His gaze flicked back to the clock. It was half past four in the morning.

He needed to get her home. She had not had the opportunity to restore her health since the sea voyage which had so violently affected her.

Leaving Lambeth's house, he knew, could leave the way clear for d'Arblier to continue his search. But how would d'Arblier know that Jack had not found what he came after?

It was a risk Jack would have to take. They couldn't stay in this room interminably. He would allow Daphne to doze a bit longer. Since he meant to return at the first possibility, he must ensure that Lambeth's body was not discovered. That meant he needed to eradicate any sign of blood on the flooring, especially in the main corridor.

For the next fifteen minutes, he set about tidying the place and tearing more fabric from the draperies to use in wiping the blood away from the floor. He was glad his wife was asleep. This wasn't the sort of thing a woman need to be exposed to.

When he finished, he went to awaken her. He paused and stared at her sweet face. The spectacles had slipped so far down her rather perfect nose that they had nearly slipped off. He pressed a gentle kiss upon her cheek, and her eyes opened.

"Oh, dear! I fell asleep."

"We've done enough for one night. I'm taking you home." He helped her get up.

"I am vastly sleepy." She stood there, pouting at him.

"Pray, what's wrong?"

"You do realize another night has passed, and we're still not properly wed."

Did she have to remind him? It was getting more difficult each day to be so close to her and not be able to possess her. He drilled her with a seductive look. "It will be worth the wait."

She let out a little squeal.

$\mathcal{C}$hapter 17

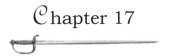

Reading other people's post was a surefire way to get drowsy. (Unless the other person was Harriette Wilson. Now, that demirep's posts would be wickedly wide-eyed reading, to be sure.) But such was certainly not the case with posts belonging to the recently departed Lord Lambeth. Daphne could not remember when she'd ever been more bored or ever sleepier than the previous night as she and Jack had sat reading Lord Lambeth's tripe in the room where he had been slain.

As she came fully awake the following morning, her first sight was of red velvet bed curtains. Which reminded her she was in Jack's bed. Beside him. She rolled over to stare at the wondrous spectacle of her husband. His dark lashes were downcast as he slumbered soundly. Her gaze lazily ran along the full length of him—though much of him was beneath the bed coverings—and her opinion that her Captain Sublime was statue-worthy was reinforced. He was a sight she never tired of.

But today she had important matters of state to see to. A quick glance at the clock told her it was just past noon. Had her brain been functioning properly at four that morning, she would never have left Lambeth House. What if the duc d'Arblier was watching and waiting for them to leave so he could search the house? With his devious mind, he was just likely to instinctively know where Lord Black Murderer was likely to have hidden secret documents.

She wasn't about to allow her ailing husband to go back to that dreadful house just yet. He did need a good night's sleep. And she was determined to have the surgeon take a look at the knife wound her husband had sustained the night before.

Since Lambeth House needed watching, she thought she knew just the person to do it. She inched out of the bed almost soundlessly, padded barefoot across the wooden floor (with only one board creaking), and slowly pulled the door open as silently as possible.

She heard the soft murmur of female voices. That would be Mrs. MacInnes and Annie. She did hope the two got along well.

In her own bedchamber, she scribbled a note and sealed it, then grabbed a handful of coins from her reticule. Without changing from her night shift, she raced—as quietly as she could—down the three flights of stairs that took her to the basement kitchen and the two female servants.

"Dearie," Mrs. MacGinnes was saying to Annie, "if you could read, you'd know that sugar is not in this bag and flour in the other." Upon hearing Daphne approach, the housekeeper spun around. Her eyes widened, and her open mouth a perfect oval. "Pray, Mrs. Dryden, you had only to ring, and I would have come to you."

Daphne knew the mistress of the house never set foot in a kitchen, but she had a great need for haste. "I must beg that you deliver a letter for me." Daphne also knew the housekeeper never performed such menial tasks.

Mrs. MacInnes' face brightened. "I will be happy to. I enjoy getting out of doors, and nothing's better than a good walk."

Daphne handed her the letter. "This must be taken immediately to my brother-in-law, Sir Ronald Johnson. His address in Whitehall is on the letter."

The housekeeper eyed the sloppy script and nodded.

"I suggest you walk over to Kings Road and take a hackney coach to The Strand." Daphne uncoiled her fist to reveal the coins in her palm. "Here's money for the coach. I'm afraid I couldn't wait while our driver readies our own conveyance." Of course, it wasn't really their own since it was hired, but for now it was theirs.

Mrs. MacInnes nodded as she took the coins. "I daresay that would set us back another twenty minutes. I'll just fetch my cloak and be on my way."

Daphne then addressed the cook. "And, Annie, I beg that you run around to the livery stable just behind us and have the coachman ready the coach for me. He's a young man by the name of Andy."

"I'll do it right now, my lady."

Later, when time was not so precious, Daphne would request that Annie, too, address her as Mrs. Dryden. But today, there was not a second to be spared. They could not give the duc the opportunity to go back and search Lambeth House.

Back in her bedchamber, Daphne donned a green muslin dress sprigged with embroidered flowers. The fabric had been a most dear expense, but Cornelia had insisted it be part of Daphne's trousseau. Daphne knew Cornelia's concern was not for the bride but for herself. The duchess was forever lamenting that Daphne was an embarrassment in the well-worn brown bombazine she preferred wearing most every day. (Brown *was* ever so practical since stains scarcely showed on it, and Daphne did have the devil of a time keeping ink stains from her garments.)

Though she hoped to return to Dryden House before Jack awakened, she ought to leave him a note explaining her whereabouts if he should wake up before she returned.

By the time she had put on the stays and stockings and bonnet, and made herself reasonably presentable, Andy had brought around the coach. She quickly addressed Annie. "I shouldn't like Captain Dryden to be disturbed from his sleep, but when you hear him stirring, I beg that you take him toast and tea.

Outside, Daphne directed Andy to return her to Manchester Square. "This time, I'll go in the front door."

"And I'll be there to protect you from Britain's enemies."

At their destination, she was pleased to see that Sir Ronald's phaeton was already there. Mrs. MacInnes was a most efficient servant.

The baronet leapt down from the phaeton as she disembarked from her coach. "What the devil's going on?" he demanded. "I was dragged away from a meeting of the privy council."

Mrs. MacInnes certainly demonstrated a stunning level of competence. "I assure you, this is massively important."

His eyes widened. "What is of such massive importance?"

She lowered her voice, and as the two of them stood upon the pavement in front of Lambeth House with all manner of conveyances clopping to and fro behind them. She sketched out the events of the previous night. "I think you will agree," she concluded, "that we cannot leave Lambeth House unwatched."

A grim set to his mouth, he nodded.

She eyed the sword at his side. "I see you followed my advice to come armed."

"Indeed."

"I pray you won't have use of it."

"What about the body?"

She froze for several seconds. "You're the government official. Surely you can think of how to deal with such. I believe if you just barge into that house with the natural authority of a baronet or the undersecretary of the Foreign Office and start throwing your weight around, the Lambeth servants will be quaking to earn your favor."

He chuckled. "Now that I know what's going on, I believe I *will* throw my weight around. In fact, I'll have some of his majesty's Horse Guards come to protect our interests here."

"Jack will be here later this afternoon. I daresay I shall have to confess that I've shared the details of our inquiry with you."

He winced. "I have a distinct feeling your husband does not like me."

Her initial tendency was to protest, but Daphne was far too honest (in most situations) to lie. The truth was that Jack *didn't* like the baronet. Why? She did not know. Ronnie was ever such a dear. "How could anyone not like you, Sir Ronald?" She favored him with her cheeriest smile as the two of them approached the front door of Lambeth House. "There is one more thing I must ask of you before I return to my husband."

"Yes?"

"If you should do something with the body, I beg that you set aside his boots. I do believe they'd do wonderfully for our coachman, who has a sad need for such."

"I thought you didn't have a coachman."

"Well, he's not precisely *ours*, but he's been with us for several days, and he's ever so dependable, and Lord Black Murderer's boots *are* of an exceedingly fine quality. I daresay they were paid for with Cornelia's blackmail payments."

"Lord Black Murderer?"

She shrugged. "First it was just Lord Blackmailer, but that didn't seem vile enough to suit him."

"I see. Because of Prufoy?"

She nodded, and her voice softened, her thoughts flicking to the man's tidy little house on Cotton Lane. "From all accounts Mr. Prufoy was a wonderful man."

"It appears his death has been avenged."

"In an odd sort of way, I suppose it has. Though the man who murdered Lord Black Murderer is even more vile than he was."

"The duc d'Arblier's only serving his country as we serve ours."

"The man will never elicit empathy from me." she spit out the words, her eyes narrowing as she spoke. "He's been bent on killing Jack for years."

"Because Captain Jack Dryden is the best England has."

His words kept the smile on her face as she left him knocking upon the door of Lambeth House. She was still smiling as Andy opened the coach door for her. But as soon as she entered the coach, she went to scream.

The aborted scream was muffled by a man's hand fiercely clasping her mouth.

The man crouched in her coach was the duc d'Arblier.

$\mathcal{C}$hapter 18

A persistent pounding upon his chamber door awakened him. His quick glance on the bed beside him told him Daphne wasn't there.

And Daphne would not be rapping at his door.

He slung his legs over the side of the bed and shimmied into his pantaloons. A pity all the servants were female. "Yes?"

Their young cook opened the door and edged into the room. "I hates to wake you, Captain, but no one's here to advise me. A lad just delivered a letter addressed to you, and he said it be urgent."

Good lord, was the girl shaking? "You did the right thing." He spoke gently as he moved to her and took the proffered letter. "Where is my wife?"

"I don't know, but she left in yer coach a 'alf hour ago." The girl's face brightened. "She left a note for you in her bedchamber."

"Thank you. That will be all." He turned over the letter and instantly recognized its seal's distinctive embossed coronet. It was d'Arblier's. He tore open the letter. As he read the few hastily written words, a chill inched down his spine like a thick, corrosive acid.

I have your wife. If you care to offer yourself in exchange for her, come alone at midnight. In

Hampstead. At the barn behind the rectory of the Methodist clergyman.

He flung the note down and hurried to Daphne's bedchamber, hoping like a simpleton that she was still there. His heartbeat stampeding, he moved to her French desk where she'd propped up the letter to him. Just as Annie had said.

Anger slammed through him as he picked it up and read.

I couldn't leave Lambeth House unguarded. I've enlisted help and will return shortly (hopefully before you awaken).

Your most obedient, adoring wife.

He gave a bitter harrumph. She was as obedient as an errant child. She was an overbearing, authoritative, arrogant firstborn who was too damned confidant for her own good!

She was the most exasperating, maddening. . .lovable woman he'd ever known.

In these past few seconds of unimaginable worry he clearly realized what mattered most to him on earth. If she had lied to him—and he had no doubts of that—she had her reasons. And he intrinsically knew they were honorable.

Like the woman he loved. The woman he would give his own life to spare.

In a furious rage, he dressed.

Even knowing what a futile effort it would be, he had to return to Lambeth House. Perhaps he could learn something there. That must be where d'Arblier had accosted her.

What about Andy? The cook had said he'd collected Daphne. Perhaps he would know something. Jack tried to tamp down his slim hopes as he made his way to the livery stable.

Neither coach nor driver was there. Though not unexpected, it was, nevertheless, disheartening.

His next destination—mounted on Warrior—was the house where Lambeth had been slain. A smile curved his lips as he remembered Daphne calling the dead viscount Lord Blackmailer.

He hoped to God he'd get to hear her voice again.

At Lambeth House, there was no sign of Andy, no sign of the coach they had hired in Portsmouth. God, but the brief time they'd been in Portsmouth—and in Spain—seemed a lifetime ago.

Curiously, there was a very fine phaeton tethered right in front of Lambeth House. He was sure he'd seen it before. Then he stiffened as he remembered who owned it.

He dismounted and stalked up to the front door—which opened before he knocked.

There, cocky as Petruchio, stood Sir Ronald Johnson in all his handsome stature. The fellow even had a gleaming sword strapped to his side!

But this was no time for petty peevishness. Only one thing mattered: saving Daphne from the clutches of the evil duc.

"Glad you've come, Captain. I suppose Lady Daphne has by now told you she has taken me into her confidence about your dashed important mission."

"I have not seen my wife. It appears the duc d'Arblier has her."

Sir Ronald gasped, his eyes wide with terror. "How could this be? I saw her no more than an hour ago."

"Where?"

"Right here! She asked that I come watch the house because she feared the duc would find the list---" He gave a little cough and lowered his voice, "and the, ah, Duchess's letters."

"Was our coachman with her?"

"I thought you didn't have a coach—oh, yes, you've hired one. Yes, I believe he was. In fact, Daf was hoping I could filch the boots from, ahem, well, you know. . ." He lowered his voice. "The deceased. Servants don't know about him yet."

"You mean he's still in the cupboard?"

The baronet nodded.

"I supposed that's as good a place as any for the blackguard."

"Lord Black Murderer," Sir Ronald said with a chuckle. "Clever little moniker your wife came up with."

Jack did not like it one bit that Daphne had used her little witticisms in front of that swaggering Sir Ronald. And he liked it even less that the womanizer referred to Jack's wife as *Daf*! Even if he was her brother-in-law.

But, of course, none of that mattered now. Jack would have to join forces with the man in the hopes of saving his wife.

What a pity! There was nothing to be done about it. Jack simply was not in good enough condition to take on the skilled French assassin.

And hope to win.

"Forgive me for getting off this most grave subject of your wife's abduction," Sir Ronald said, slinging an arm around Jack. "You must tell me everything."

Before they crossed the threshold of Lambeth House, though, a great skidding of coach wheels sounded on the street behind them, and they turned to see a second carriage bearing the baronet's crest come to a halt, and Lady Virginia leaping from the conveyance, her eyes narrowed. "Where is that lying, cheating, stealing, former old maid sister of mine?"

* * *

The sister in question, her hands tied behind her, was reposing on an upper floor of a warehouse in London's East End. Had that blasted duc bought up all the menacing-looking, derelict warehouses that lined the quays along the River Thames?

At sword point, she and Andy had been forced to climb two rickety flights of dark stairs and were locked behind a well-bolted door in a musty, unfurnished room with boarded windows. Transoms well above the windows—far too high for them to even touch—had not been boarded, an omission which, to Daphne's gratitude, kept the chamber from being dark.

She was too much reminded of the last time she'd been foolish enough to be abducted by the duc d'Arblier. That time, though, she'd been captured by one of the man's minions. This time the duc did not entrust the deed to an underling.

The underling was used to capture poor Andy, who now sat across from her in the dark chamber that likely had not been set foot in for a generation, his hands also bound behind him. The poor lad, who couldn't be eighteen yet, must be terrified. Even if he thought he had the makings of a Bow Street Runner. Or spy.

"I am vastly sorry that you've been captured merely because of your association with me," she said. "I do have the utmost confidence my husband will save us from the evil duc's clutches."

Since Jack wasn't there, she had no qualms about using the adjectives that so aptly described the man she had married. "Captain Dryden, I must tell you, is on a special mission for the Prince Regent. That is because he's been master spy against the French in the Peninsular campaigns."

Andy's fair blue eyes widened. "A mission for the Regent 'imself? A master spy? Wait 'till I tell me mum."

Swelling with pride, Daphne nodded. She certainly hoped he would live to tell his mother. There was the consideration that Jack wasn't his usual, masterful self. Physically. All because of that odious duc! "This same French mastermind who captured us actually abducted us several weeks ago, but my brilliant husband managed to extricate us. We—my husband and I—were able to stop a plot to kill the Regent."

"Blimy!"

"It's all true. The Prince Regent wanted to give Captain Dryden a big fancy Lord Something title, but my humble husband refused."

Andy's eyes widened even more. "Blimy! A plot to murder the Regent? This could be in a 'orace Walpole book! And now yer being charged with capturing Frenchie spies! You and the cap'n."

"We must obtain a list of counterspies operating within the highest levels of British government."

He whistled.

She was relieved that her diversion had taken the lad's mind off his fear. "I believe our captor believes we've already found the list, and we need him to continue believing that."

"'e won't 'ear otherwise from me. I'll take the secret to me grave, I will."

"Very good, Andy. I knew I could count on you."

* * *

Jack gathered his wife's hysterical sister and her husband, and steered them into the dead viscount's library. Slamming the door behind them, he raised his voice. "If either of you give a fig about the wonderful woman I married, then for God's sake put your silliness aside and help me rescue her." He leveled a stern gaze at Daphne's whimpering sister. "You do Daphne a great disservice if you think she would ever betray you." His gaze shifted to Sir Ronald. "Oblige us both by explaining why you and my wife have been meeting in so clandestine a fashion."

Sir Ronald turned to Virginia. "You knew about that?"

Her weeping eyes met his, and she nodded.

The baronet took hold of both his wife's hands and spoke tenderly. "Never doubt my love of—or my fidelity to—you. Lady Daphne needed my assistance on a matter that she and the captain are investigating for the Foreign Office."

"Why such secrecy?" Jack asked.

Sir Ronald directed his gaze to Jack. "You knew I was meeting with Lady Daphne?"

Jack nodded ruefully.

Drawing in a deep sigh, Sir Ronald continued. "She didn't want you to know."

"Know what?" Jack's eyes narrowed.

"That she asked me to undertake a portion of the investigation that neither of you were. . . ah, equipped to undertake." Sir Ronald offered Jack a smile, then continued. "What was needed was a man who had entre into the men's clubs. Your wife did not want you to think that she found you lacking in any manner—especially in a manner which might call attention to your---"

"My lack of social connections?"

"Precisely. So early in your marriage, she particularly did not want you to feel . . . for lack of a better word, unworthy of her. She wanted nothing to point to any disparity in your stations."

Jack had instinctively known that whatever secret she was keeping from him was done for a good reason. And what better reason than preserving harmony in their marriage? He met the baronet's serious gaze. "So my wife wished for you to see if any member of one of your clubs had recently come into money?"

"She did."

"I don't understand," Virginia said.

Sir Ronald told his wife about the missing list, the two murders, and last, he told her about her twin's purloined love letters.

She began to bawl. "My poor sister. That wretched, vile, disgusting, murdering duc has my dear sister! Oh, Ronnie, you must get her back."

Sir Ronald nodded, a firm set to his jaw as he made eye contact with Jack. "How do you know the duc has her?"

Jack thrust the letter at him.

With his wife peering over his shoulder, Sir Ronald quickly read the letter. "You'll need my help, Dryden. You're in no condition to defend yourself, much less rescue your wife."

"I will be glad of your help. Obviously, she's not being held at that barn. It would be too easy for us to gather up some of his majesty's Horse Guards and storm the place. My guess is they're bringing her there later."

"And obviously the duc means to kill you." Sir Ronald turned to his wife. "My dearest love, we shall need you to carry on with the search for the duchess's letters. You know her hand so very well, you're the very one to set about searching this house."

She turned up her nose. "Are we not going to do anything about the. . ." She lowered her voice. "The body?"

"Not yet. We need to carry on with the search. I've told the servants to expect soldiers because French spies have targeted this house. And I told them that any of them who wished to leave, had permission to do so."

"Did any stay?"

"Only two. The housekeeper and cook. Both females." He chuckled. "All the males fled."

"The Horse Guards really are coming?" Jack asked.

"I sent a note round. Of course, it was not written on my official stationary, which I expect has delayed things a bit. It's my intention to keep two men posted at the front and two more at the back as a deterrent to the duc."

Jack frowned. "The pity of it is if d'Arblier sees that, he will know we haven't found the list. It's rather like showing him our hand."

"It has just occurred to me that if I send them away it could demonstrate that we already have the list—in which case, the need to murder you might decrease."

"Anything that decreases my chances of being murdered is certainly to be desired, but d'Arblier would be bound to know the truth because the men on the list have continued unimpeded."

Sir Ronald's gaze swept over the library. "Which rooms have you and Daphne already searched?"

"This room was completely searched last night, but I see the servants have been busy today restoring the books we'd flung to the floor." Jack nodded in the direction of the viscount's study. "In the next chamber, which is—or should I say, was—Lambeth's study, we spent several hours going through papers but did not finish. We left at four this morning. I'd better finish that myself. Later. Now all that matters is getting my wife away from that fiend."

Sir Ronald pecked his wife on the cheek. "Go along to the other chambers, my darling. "I have confidence you can find the letters."

A smile on her face, her brow lowered in concentration, she left the chamber.

"I didn't want to say this in from of my wife," Sir Ronald said. "You know how wives worry."

Jack nodded, now ashamed of himself for distrusting his wife.

"I think the fact the switch has been scheduled for midnight will be of tremendous advantage for us."

"Why?" Jack asked.

"Because it will be very dark. You and I are built most similarly. A hood about my head and I daresay even our wives won't know the difference. From a distance."

Jack had most seriously misjudged the man who stood before him, offering his own life to save Daphne. No wonder Sir Ronald had been so intent on removing Virginia from the room. No matter how much she loved her sister, she wouldn't want her husband to use himself in such deadly barter. If she'd been hysterical before, she would be prostrate on learning of her husband's noble offer. "I can't allow you to endanger your life in such a manner. You just said the duc means to murder me."

"I don't intend to be killed. You'll come along behind me and save the day, don't you know."

"The two of us would be outnumbered. I'm almost certain d'Arblier hired the three cutthroats who attacked me at the public house, and there's no way of knowing how many others he employs."

"I'm counting on your element of surprise being the weapon that tips the scales in our favor."

Jack could understand Sir Ronald's logic. "Today we must do reconnaissance." The success of any mission lay in precision planning. Before they set foot near that barn tonight, Jack aimed to know every square foot of land within a one-mile radius of it.

"You're too well known to them," Sir Ronald said. "Leave it to me. In daylight my blond hair will set me far apart from you. Besides, I have many friends in Hampstead who may be of assistance."

A female screamed. This was not an oh-goodness-I-just-saw-a-mouse scream. This was the kind of scream that came from one witnessing a gruesome death.

$\mathcal{C}$hapter 19

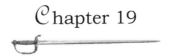

The Lambeth housekeeper stood in the grand hallway of Lambeth House screaming and crying at the same time. "My master! My master! Oh, please, someone, help!"

Jack's gaze swept from the distraught, middle-aged woman to the Elizabethan sideboard in which a lone door stood open, and Lambeth's soft leather boot—a rather stiff leg attached to it— protruded. He fleetingly thought of filching the boots for poor Andy and hoped to God the lad hadn't been slain by the same fiend who killed Lambeth.

His first instinct was to comfort the housekeeper, but he realized such an action would betray that he had known the viscount had been murdered and stuffed there. Better to appear shocked and dismayed.

With Sir Ronald at his heels, he stormed up to the sideboard, and peered into the dark, bloodied opening before looking back at the hysterical woman. "I take it this poor creature is Lord Lambeth?"

Her teary eyes wide, she nodded.

"Demmed Frenchies," Sir Ronald said before begging the woman's pardon for his foul language. Jack rather admired what a gifted actor Sir Ronald was proving to be.

"A pity we did not learn of the threat in time to prevent this unfortunate deed." Jack was tearing a page from Sir Ronald's rather brilliant script.

Virginia, her shaky hand clasped to her mouth, stood at the top of the stairs peering down at them. "How dreadful." Then she hurried down the stairs and put her arm around the housekeeper. "Come, my dear woman, and sit down. I'll have cook prepare you a cup of tea."

"I should have left when the others did," the whimpering woman said. "It's a wonder I wasn't murdered."

"But, gratefully, you were not." The tenderness in Virginia's voice reminded Jack of what Daphne had told him about her nurturing sister.

God, he was worried sick about Daphne. He hadn't been so low since Edwards had been murdered.

"Do, love," Sir Ronald said to his wife, "find out if she knows a kinsman of Lord Lambeth. Someone will have to make the proper arrangements. . ."

Once the women were in the drawing room, Jack and Sir Ronald began to plan. The baronet would rush to Hampstead immediately to familiarize himself with the terrain, and the two would meet at Primrose Hill in three hours to discuss their next move.

They decided to stay with the plan to have Horse Guards watch Lambeth House, Jack suspected because Sir Ronald knew he would not be able to get his wife away, and he was not about to leave her at Lambeth House unprotected.

Jack had his own plans for the next three hours. As soon as the Horse Guards arrived, he mounted Warrior and rode fast and hard to the Foreign Office.

When he arrived, he stalked past Lord Castlereagh's office and continued climbing stairs until he reached the top floor and the small office of Harold Martin. The well-dressed silver-haired man gazed up at Jack, and a broad smile brightened his face. "Well, if it isn't the best spy in the history of England," he said, as he got to his feet and came to shake Jack's hand.

Jack was inordinately pleased over the man's praise. If Daphne had said those words, it would have bothered him. Before today. Now, if he could just see her, he wouldn't care what words streamed from her mouth.

"It's you, Martin, who's the best there ever was. In fact, that's why I'm here today. I need to bring the master of disguise out of retirement."

"There's nothing I wouldn't do for you, Captain. Tell me what you need."

* * *

When Sir Ronald rode his mount half way up Primrose Hill three hours later, his brows elevated at what he saw. The normally well-dressed Harold Martin—with whom he often worked at the Foreign Office—sat on the box of a hay cart, shabbily dressed and stoop shouldered. Beside him Jack was dressed all in black with a sword at his side.

"A plan is in the germination stage, but I need to know everything you learned today," Jack said to Sir Ronald.

Sir Ronald greeted Martin, then addressed Jack. "Most of my friends in Hampstead are not acquainted with the Methodists, but one of them lives fairly close to the Methodist preacher—I

believe that is what he's called. He said the
preacher, whose name is Douglas Douglass." He
held up his hands. "I am not making this up! Well,
Douglas Douglass was called away to his married
daughter's who is gravely ill. He and his wife left,
and the house has been dark for the past couple
of days. No one's there, nor is there anyone in the
barn. I checked."

Jack nodded. "It rather makes one think the
duc must be close to someone in the vicinity."

"I thought the same thing," Sir Ronald said. "I
asked if any French émigrés lived nearby, but the
answer was negative."

"What about disreputables?"

"My friend said to his knowledge there weren't
any really bad sorts about, but there were some
pretty pathetic gin-soakers."

"You found out where?"

"I did, but they haven't been home in the past
few days."

"They could very well be Daphne's captors.
Which means they could be anywhere in the
Greater London area."

"But one thing's certain," Sir Ronald said.

Jack raised a single brow in query. "What?"

"They'll be in Hampstead tonight."

A solemn look on his face, Jack nodded. "I
brought pen and paper in the hopes you can draw
for me the barn and the area around it."

For the next half hour Sir Ronald told Jack
everything he needed to know.

"From what you're telling me," Jack said, "I
think my plan just might work."

"Enlighten me, please," Sir Ronald said.

"It's likely someone is watching the barn today, wouldn't you say?" Jack's gaze fanned from Martin to Sir Ronald.

Both men nodded.

"I think I know what you're planning," Sir Ronald said, eying the hay cart. "You're going to hide beneath that hay, aren't you, Dryden?"

Jack nodded.

"And this harmless old, silver-haired man will be seen delivering hay to the barn belonging to Douglas Douglass," Sir Ronald continued.

"No one will be able to see Captain Dryden leave the cart because I'll have it scooted just inside the barn door," Martin said. "He gets out of the cart and hides beneath hay once more inside the barn."

"What if they find him tonight? Before they bring Lady Daphne or when they first bring her?" Sir Ronald asked.

Jack shrugged. "I have a knife as well as a sword." He swallowed and gazed at his brother-in-law. "If they kill me, I'm counting on you to save Daphne."

"I give you my word." Sir Ronald looked at Martin. "Can we count on your help?"

"You couldn't keep me away."

"I am not fooled by your gray hair," Sir Ronald said. "Past your prime you may be, but you're an uncommonly skilled swordsman. I propose to have you stay at my friend's who lives near the Methodist preacher in Hampstead. I'll give you a letter of introduction."

"Will I be able to see the barn under tonight's three-quarter moon?"

"You will."

"Then if you need help, I will be there."

For the next hour Jack and his brother-in-law made their plans with the precision of a most disciplined architect.

$\mathcal{C}$hapter 20

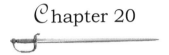

Daphne hadn't the heart to tell Andy that Jack's previous rescues had been conducted when he was in prime physical condition. That, sadly, was no longer the case. His ribs were broken, his shoulder was incapable of movement, and his knee was so swollen he could hardly put his weight upon it. Some help he would be!

But for the lad's sake, she must keep up the illusion that invincible Jack would save them from the murderous French duc.

The room they were being held in had gone almost completely dark after the sun set. She had no way of knowing the time. When there was nothing with which to occupy oneself, each minute was like ten. Or twenty. She calculated it must be ten or eleven, judging from when the last rays of light shone through the transom before it had gone dark.

Though she could no longer see Andy clearly, she could picture the strapping lad who was all dangly arms and legs with little meat on those elongated bones. She fancied Jack might have been similarly slender when he'd been that age. It would have taken a few years for the musculature to develop on that tall body.

Her pulse accelerated at the memory of Jack's sublime body, of lying beside him on the red velvet bed, of wanting to make love to the man she had pledged herself to in a sacramental ceremony.

A fog horn sounded some little distance away, confirming her suspicion they were being kept in a warehouse in the Docklands. Memories crashed over her of that last time the duc had kept her prisoner in a warehouse that was likely located near this one. She had cried that time because she didn't want to go to her grave a virgin. Now she was a married woman, and the same fear brought tears to her eyes.

She must reverse the morbid direction of her thoughts. "Tell me, Andy, do you ever fight?"

"What kind of fightin' might ye be referring to, me lady?"

"Fisticuffs, actually."

"I wouldn't want ye to be thinking of me as a 'othead. Me mum always said because I was big, I couldn't go beatin' other fellows up. *Turn the other cheek*, she always told me, but sometimes a bit of fightin' is unavoidable."

"Oh, I can tell you're ever so obliging. I know you would never initiate a physical confrontation. In the same way, I know you wouldn't back away from one, either."

"That be a fact, me lady."

"It has occurred to me you might be able to assist my husband when he tries to rescue us."

"How? I can't do nothing as long as me hands is tied behind me."

"Then we shall have to see if there's some way to remove the rope. If you could figure out a way to untie mine, then I would be at liberty to untie yours. I say this only because I believe you are much more capable of undoing my ropes than I am of yours."

"Let's give it a go." He began to scoot toward her.

"Should you prefer me seated or lying on my stomach?"

"Seated should be good enough." He drew so close she could feel his body heat. Next, she felt his knuckles brushing against her hands as he fumbled with the knots of her rope. This went on for several minutes. She kept hoping he would emerge victorious from his task, but five minutes dragged into ten, then into twenty—she was quite sure, even though she had no way of telling time. The poor lad kept mumbling unpleasantries under his breath as each new attempt came up without success.

But he would not give up.

She ignored the hemp burns scratching her flesh. When weighed against the prospect of release, a bit of raw flesh was most negligible.

After a very long time, Andy decided to try a different approach. "I believe I'll try to bite through the rope. The knots must 'av been tied by sailors 'cause they're near impossible to undo."

"Come to think of it, my husband thought the men who attacked him the other night might have been sailors, and I have no doubts they were hired by the wicked Frenchman who abducted us."

She hated to discourage Andy when hope was all they had. But the likelihood of gnawing through one-inch rope with human teeth was most improbable. "I do hope your teeth are strong."

"They better be. I'll be chewing for our lives."

So he did know how bleak were their prospects.

"I am ever so sorry for involving you, Andy. You were just trying to do an honest day's work, and fate has pitted you against the most vile spy France has."

He spit out a mouthful of hemp fibers. "I mean to get us out of 'ere. The captain will need me assistance."

She sighed. "Indeed he will, Andy." She had no regrets about encouraging the fellow. The mood he was in now was much preferable than the melancholy which had beset him that afternoon. Now he possessed hope, and as long as he possessed hope he had the determination to at least try to get them out of that horrid place and away from the duc's reach. "My husband said the success of any mission is in precision planning; therefore, my lad, we must begin to plan."

He lifted his head from his gnawing-mouse imitation and spoke excitedly. "I was thinking, me lady, that after ye get the ropes off me, I would pretend they was still on---"

"Andy, my brilliant young man! That is exactly what I was going to suggest."

"That way, when the wicked Frenchie comes for ye, I can wait until just the right moment to try to save ye."

"My guess is that he's offering to release me in exchange for my husband." A little whimper escaped. "Oh, Andy, I couldn't live—wouldn't want to—without my Jack. You must keep the Frenchman from killing him."

He lifted his head and spat out another mouthful of the rope's fibers. "I shall do me best. Pity I won't have a weapon."

It was a dashed pity that neither of them would ever be free of these wretched ropes. But she would keep up the pretense. "Let us concentrate on things we can control."

"I don't mean to boast, but I'm a good fighter, but only with me fists. I ain't never held a sword in me hand."

"Then to even the fight, you must steal your guard's weapon when he's unaware. I've seen you with the horses. You have very quick reflexes."

"I 'ope I'm quick enough." He paused and attempted to spit away the chunks of hemp. "Me mum says everything 'appens for a reason. The Lord must 'av put me in Lunnon so as I could help you and the captain."

"I hope so, Andy. I hope so."

All of a sudden her hands were free! She spun around and threw her arms around her liberator. "You succeeded! How wonderful!"

"No time for celebrating, me lady. Ye need to untie me."

Given that it was dark, it was difficult to untie knots she couldn't see, but at least she had the use of both of her hands. In front of her. Within a few minutes, she managed to untie the knots and free him, too, of the ropes.

He set about retying hers, then merely encircled his again with the gnawed-through rope to give the illusion his hands were tied behind him.

"Remember what my husband says about planning."

"The success of a mission is in precision planning."

"Very good, Andy! Now, what is our plan?"

"I'm to look as if I'm tied up until there is a danger either to ye or to ye 'usband. Then me first act will be to quickly try to disarm the person making the threat to you."

"The minute I perceive a threat, I will attempt to distract the duc's attention away from the direction where you are. Perhaps I can wail and collapse at his feet."

"Perhaps is not precision."

Thank her stars Andy was intelligent. "You are right. Allow me to rephrase. As soon as I perceive a threat to me or my husband, I *will* wail and collapse at the duc's feet."

"And the instant you wail, I attack."

Horse hooves pounded three stories below them. They hadn't heard a single clomp all night. Instead of dying away, the clomping halted. Close. Her heartbeat thundered. *The duc!*

But the person who raced up the stairs to the room where they were being held wasn't him. It was one of his hired English henchman, whom she was almost certain was a former sailor—and one of the three men who tried to kill Jack. He unbolted the lock and threw it open. "Out! And don't attempt to get away from us, or you'll get a knife through yer heart."

They wouldn't kill her. Not yet. They would want to keep her alive until Jack saw her. But what of Andy? Their captors had no reason to keep him alive. Likewise, they had no reason to kill him, either.

She followed Andy down two flights of stairs and through the open door on the ground floor. In the moonlight she saw the duc d'Arblier mounted on a black stallion. He was dressed all in black, his hooded cape covering his head. "Pray, Hudson, help the lady mount. It's most difficult without the use of her hands."

A second man, who had been guarding the ground floor door, stepped forward and helped

Daphne onto the other horse. "No side saddle for you," the duc said to her, his voice sinister. "You'll sit the horse in the same way a man does."

Once she was mounted, the disgustingly dirty Hudson climbed up behind her. His thighs formed a V to close around her, sickening her.

"Do not think about calling for help, Lady Daphne," the duc said. "Hudson has orders to slit your throat if you try.

D'Arblier's head turned slightly while he addressed the other underling. "Wait a few minutes, then come along to the barn in Hampstead. And. . .kill the coachman."

* * *

Lying on the damp earth beneath a six foot tall pile of hay was not one of Jack's favorite experiences. But he'd certainly experienced worse during his years in clandestine operations. Perhaps the worst was when he'd had to lie at the bottom of cart full of manure in order to sneak into the French camp where Edwards was being held.

A smile crossed Jack's (rather itchy) face as he recalled his success at rescuing his best friend. Efforts to deodorize his uniform, though, failed utterly. He'd ended up having to burn the foul-smelling thing.

Earlier that evening, he had taken one of the two knives on his person and carved out a wedge from the barn wall near the only entrance. He had waited until it was dark to perform his extraction so that he would be able to see the rural landscape fanning around the barn's entrance. He wanted to be able to determine if someone else were being sent there to lie in wait for him—or for the man they expected to be him.

It was beastly decent of Sir Ronald to offer himself for so dangerous a mission. If it were merely for his own sake, Jack would never have allowed the baronet to make such a sacrifice. The man, after all, had a family and children to consider.

But with Daphne's life at risk, there was nothing Jack wouldn't do, no risk he wouldn't take, no other life he would preserve over hers.

The knowledge that her meetings with Sir Ronald—and her lies—had been calculated purely to preserve Jack's own pride made his heart swell with love for the woman he had married.

He had waited until past eleven before he crawled beneath the haystack to lie in wait.

Since the day he had entered the army, it seemed as if Jack had spent half his time waiting. As he lie there in near total darkness, the minutes dragged. His heightened sense of hearing compensated for the loss of sight.

But nothing compensated for the tedium.

At last he heard the soft pound of distant horses. More than one. They would be there soon.

Two or three minutes later horses drew up in front of the barn. No matter how many times Jack had faced imminent danger, his heartbeat always stampeded like it was doing now. His palms sweat. And—even though he normally had great confidence in his own abilities—he would find himself beseeching his Maker to protect him.

The massive barn door rolled open, and the barn was no longer in total darkness. Whoever opened the door must have a lantern.

Then Jack heard the duc d'Arblier's heavily accented voice. "Check the barn. Make sure no one's hiding there. Look everywhere." His tone sharpened. "And I mean everywhere."

$\mathcal{C}$hapter 21

This was much worse than the last time she'd been held captive by the duc d'Arblier. The last time Jack had been his usual, competent, fit self. Now—thanks to that vile duc—Jack was but a fragment of his former self. The heartbreaking reality was that Jack wouldn't hesitate to put himself in harm's way in order to protect her. And in harm's way in his present condition would mean almost certain death.

She could weep. Complete happiness had been within their grasp. Soon she would likely lose her life before fully experiencing it. As would Andy. Poor, dear boy. The notion of Jack's mighty body stilled by death brought uncontrollable tears.

"Your husband awaits us in Hampstead," the duc had told her not long after she'd mounted. "He is offering himself in exchange for you."

Exactly as she had thought. Her tears thickened.

"But you're not a man whose word can be trusted," she had told him. "You will kill us both."

D'Arblier gave a wicked laugh. "A pity you know me so well, my lady."

"I fail to see any humor in the fact you're devoid of honor."

"You malign me because I serve my country?"

"My husband serves his country, too, but he has never sacrificed his honor. I don't believe you ever possessed any."

When they reached the outskirts of London, then the rural area of Hampstead, her pulse accelerated. How she wanted to see Jack once more, but not now, not when two armed men meant to kill him.

Soon they were quietly clopping along the village of Hampstead's main street. An old half-timbered inn with a single window lighted looked as if it would provide a warm, comforting haven for weary travelers. The aroma of wood fires—so much more inviting than the coal fires of London—impressed upon her a vision of a cozy little candlelit bedchamber with a fire blazing in its hearth. An overpowering desire to be there with her husband nearly consumed her.

A cool, brisk wind rocked the inn's freshly painted sign. *Feathers and Leather. Fresh horses. Good food. Clean Rooms.*

Lost in melancholy, she was surprised a moment later when the duc and the man named Hudson brought their horses to a halt in front of a barn that was in total darkness. No houses were close, save one in which all the windows were dark. She would not be surprised to learn the duc had selected this barn because he had knowledge that whoever owned it was no longer living there.

Hudson dismounted, lit a lantern, and entered the barn, his other hand clasping a knife. What if Jack were hiding there? Would they just kill him outright?

Knowing d'Arblier, Daphne felt he would want to find out if Jack had discovered the list before he killed him.

Their insurance against being swiftly murdered had hinged upon the duc's belief that Jack knew where Heffington's list was.

Her heartbeat drummed. The duc was bound to know they had *not* found it. Had they, the English traitors whose names were on that piece of paper would have been exposed.

In the distance, a lone horse cantered in their direction. She spun around. The rider was not close yet, and it was very dark, but she was almost certain the tall, well-built rider was Jack. He was dressed all in black, with a flowing cape and a hood over his head. As he drew closer, she recognized Warrior.

"You should allow me to get off this horse," she said. "It will show your good faith in making an exchange."

"Very well. We'll both stand." The duc dismounted first, then helped her down.

"Will you not remove the ropes from my wrists?" she asked.

"I think not."

"I'm sure my husband will demand it."

"I might then oblige him." The duc watched as Jack came closer.

When Jack got to within twenty feet, he stopped. "I demand that you untie my wife's hands."

It wasn't Jack! It was Sir Ronald pretending to be Jack! Her melancholy vanished. Now they might have a chance! The baronet possessed the same skills that Jack possessed when he was healthy.

This must mean that Jack was near, planning to assist Sir Ronald. Her stomach plunged. What if he were hiding in the barn?

Hudson was sure to murder him.

When the duc d'Arblier failed to respond, Sir Ronald threatened. "You had better, d'Arblier." While his voice was nothing like Jack's—though the duc hadn't been around Jack enough to remember the timbre of his voice—he spoke with the exact air of arrogance Jack would have used.

The duc unsheathed his knife.

Her heartbeat galloped. What if he used the knife to kill Sir Ronald?

Then he turned to her and began to slice through the ropes. Exhaling the mammoth breath she had been holding, Daphne edged away from the duc ever so slowly, angling herself in order to get a view of the inside of the barn. Her stomach plummeted when she saw Hudson grab the pitchfork and begin to stab the tall haystack.

"Come this way, my love," Sir Ronald said to her.

"First, captain," d'Arblier said, "I must insist that you dismount."

Sir Ronald got off Warrior. Daphne was surprised the stallion had allowed anyone besides Jack to ride him. The two were most attached. "Now my wife will mount my horse, and you will allow her to ride off."

"You know I can't allow that."

"Then we cannot come to terms."

Daphne continued walking toward her husband's horse.

"Stop!" the duc yelled, "or I'll run you through with my sword." She caught the gleam of his sword as it was being drawn, the partial moon illuminating it.

She halted abruptly.

"You will allow her to ride away," Sir Ronald hissed. "If you don't, I won't tell you with whom I've entrusted Heffington's list."

The sound of a door slamming in the distance caught her attention, and nearly simultaneously, the pounding of hooves came closer. She looked up to see two male riders racing toward them from the house that was closest to the barn.

"Your men?" Sir Ronald asked the duc.

"Of course. Surely you didn't think I was cocky enough to think I could bring you down without assistance."

"Another of his men is in the barn," she told him.

Sir Ronald sounded disgusted. "So it's to be four against one?"

"I leave nothing to chance. And soon it will be five to one. Another of my . . . employees is coming from the East End, from the spot where I've kept your wife. He had a little problem to dispose of first."

Her insides felt sickeningly like they had aboard the HMS *Avalon*. Only worse. *Poor Andy.*

"You told me I was to come alone. I've done what was asked of me."

"Yes, your wife was just telling me how honorable you are and how lacking in honor I am." With a movement so quick she almost missed it, he thrust his sword toward Sir Ronald, then put his weight on his heels as Sir Ronald drew his weapon.

Where was Jack? She moved quickly to Warrior and began to stroke the beast's mane.

Her gaze bounced from one armed man to the other. She was struck by how similarly the two had dressed, both in all black and both with hoods over their heads. Of course, the duc was considerably shorter than Jack, er, Sir Ronald.

Suddenly, she realized she, too, had been fooled. She'd only seen the duc once before today. Because this imposter was the same size as the duc and because he spoke with authority in his heavy French accent, she had assumed he was the duc d'Arblier. Now she knew with certainty it was not d'Arblier.

Was the real duc one of the men riding toward them now? Surely he would want to be near. He would not relinquish the opportunity to orchestrate matters.

He also was bound to know how important he was to his cause. France could not afford to lose him.

She addressed her brother-in-law. "Sir Ronald, this man's an imposter!"

"Sir Ronald?" the imposter queried. "Where's Jack Dryden?"

"Right here," Jack said, emerging from the barn, his sword drawn. He, too, was dressed all in black.

Her heartbeat roared. Tears of joy surged.

The Frenchman jerked around to face Jack. "Where's Hudson?"

"I regret to inform you he ran into my knife." There was not the slightest remorse in Jack's voice.

"I may not be d'Arblier, but I'm willing to fight to the death for my country!" He lunged at Jack.

Sir Ronald came to close in on him, but before he got there, the other two men had leapt from their horses, whipped out their own swords, and attacked Sir Ronald. It was too dark for Daphne to determine if either of the men was the duc.

Though she did not like that poor Ronnie had to fight off *two* men, she worried far more about her injured husband. It would be difficult for him to take on a lone man in his condition. She must help him!

She hurried to the barn. She intended to get her hands on Hudson's sword, even if it meant taking it from his dead body.

* * *

"Daphne!" Jack thundered. "Get on Warrior and get the hell out of here."

"In just one minute, my darling," she called over her shoulder as she hurried into the barn.

His wife could be most vexing.

The fraction of a second he had taken his eye off the Frenchman had been long enough for the man to close in and prick Jack with the blade of his sword. Fortunately, the blade got partially tangled in the voluminous folds of Jack's cape, but his assailant managed to extract it in a matter of seconds.

Jack lunged toward him, but the sudden impact to his injured knee sent him collapsing. He quickly sprang to his feet as the Frenchman dove to the ground, face first. On the way down, a pitchfork hurled from behind missed the Frenchman but caught his cloak.

How easy it would be for Jack to plunge his saber through his back. But Jack couldn't do that. Sword poised, he waited for the Frenchman to throw off the cloak which was now impaled into the ground and regain his position.

Now it would be a fair fight, and Jack meant to be the victor. They faced off in the clearing in front of the barn, both men thrusting and parrying, metal clashing. And Daphne screaming. Or was it shrieking?

Thank God it was his left shoulder—and not the right—that wouldn't budge. His injuries did not impede his swift attacks.

Fighting at night was bloody difficult. One stumble over uneven earth could mean death. He hoped to God it wasn't his death.

The crazed Frenchman was doing his best to drive his blade into Jack's heart.

Jack fleetingly thought of Sir Ronald. All of his reputed skill might be necessary to bring down two opponents. If only Jack could disable this man so he could assist the baronet.

Jack's blade slashed through the air; the other man parried. Back and forth. Though the Frenchman was possessed of physical attributes, he was in want of skill.

Soon Jack had him backed into the wall of the barn. Though he had no doubt the man would have killed him were Jack against that wall, Jack had no desire to deprive him of life. *The duc d'Arblier would have been a different matter.* "Daphne!" he called as the point of his blade centered on the man's chest. "I need rope."

"*Merci*," the man said, dropping his sword.

"I saw rope in the barn," she answered, whirling around and hastening back into the barn. Her voice no longer sounded hysterical.

As she was returning with a spool of rope, a sudden pounding of hooves and rattling of carriage wheels drew their attention.

Jack recognized the approaching coach as the one they had hired in Portsmouth. And Andy was up on the box, but he wasn't driving. As they drew nearer, Jack could see that Andy held a dagger on the driver, who was one of the men who'd attacked Jack at the White Lion.

The carriage pulled up five feet from them. "Me lady!" Andy called as he quickly slashed the reins, leaving the other man shaking his head and holding severed ribbons while Andy jumped from the coachman's box. "I beg that you find a way to tie up this bloke so I can 'elp you and the captain." With the knife still leveled at the man on the box, Andy ordered him to jump down.

"Here," Jack said to Andy, "get this man's saber from the ground and guard him—as well as your man—with it. I must assist Sir Ronald."

Andy ordered his captive to stand beside the Frenchman, then he plucked the sword and directed it at the two men.

Sword in hand, Jack whirled around. "Your fight is with me!" He came to plant his boots next to the baronet, drawing off one of Sir Ronald's opponents. Now solo, the man's skills were so lacking, Jack quickly backed his man into the side of the barn. When he realized he was beaten, the man threw down his weapon. "Have mercy on me, fer God's sake."

"Daphne, my love, can you get more rope?" Jack asked.

Less than a moment later, Sir Ronald had disarmed his man, who was on the verge of tears.

"Have you a spot more rope, Lady Daphne?" Sir Ronald asked.

"You're next in order," she said as she handed a length of rope to Andy, who sliced it with his knife.

Jack addressed the three men who lined the wall like stumps on a log, their hands tied. "If you don't want to end up with your throats slashed, you'd best tell me where d'Arblier is."

The last man tied was the first to speak. "He told Frenchie there he'd be sailing away on the River Thames tonight at the same time his imposter was to meet with you. And that's the honest truth."

The Frenchman began cursing in his native tongue. Obviously, the duc hadn't wanted his departure to be known.

"Where did he keep his ship?" Jack asked.

"Not more than two-hundred yards from the building where we kept the lady and the tall lad."

"Damn!" Jack hissed. "There's no way I could have a chance of getting there in time!"

Daphne turned to Andy. "However did you get away from your executioner?"

"Just like we talked about, me lady. I waited until the danger was about to commence, then I surprised him by lunging at him and relieving him of the knife."

"How did you get out of those ropes?" his former captor asked.

"'Tis a secret."

"I think it was very clever of you to make him drive you here," Daphne said to Andy.

Jack suddenly became aware of another pair of horses racing toward them. Surely it was the duc!

As they drew nearer, he saw that one of the riders was a veiled woman. All of his attention was focused upon the man, upon trying to determine if it were the duc. As the horses came closer, he heard Virginia's voice. "Oh, Ronnie, I was so worried about you!"

"How in the blazes did you know I was here?" her husband asked.

Virginia dismounted without any assistance and threw herself into her husband's arms. "I did see the captain's note from the duc d'Arblier, and I knew it would be up to you to save my sister."

Sir Ronald's gaze flipped to the man accompanying his wife.

It was Martin.

"How in the bloody hell did you end up with my wife?" he asked.

"I'm dreadfully sorry, Sir Ronald," Martin said. "I tried to dissuade her once I intercepted her riding rather hell-bent, if you know what I mean, but the lady was not to be deterred. Therefore, I thought I'd best accompany her in case she needed protection."

"Then it seems I am indebted to you," Sir Ronald said.

Daphne stepped toward her sister.

"Thank God Ronnie rescued you." Virginia hugged Daphne, then she turned to the others. "You will be happy to know I found . . ." She lowered her voice. "Ahem, Cornelia's letters at Lambeth House."

"Where?" Daphne asked.

"They were tied with pink ribbon and placed in a dressing table drawer of the deceased Viscountess Lambeth."

"You didn't find anything . . . else?" Jack asked, settling a possessive arm around Daphne.

"No." Virginia turned back to her husband and lifted her face to his.

"Now, dearest," Sir Ronald said, "Mr. Martin and I must take these ruffians to prison."

"I'm not letting you out of my sight!"

"Very well, my love," Sir Ronald said. "You'll come with us."

While they were kissing, Daphne turned and gazed up adoringly at her own husband. "I am so proud of you, my love."

"There's nothing to be proud of. I failed to get d'Arblier, and I couldn't save my own wife without assistance." He hung his head. "Sir Ronald's the hero."

"Sir Ronald did *not* have a useless shoulder, injured knee, or broken ribs! *You* were magnificent!" She reached up to tenderly stroke his cheek. "I know it wasn't easy for you to accept assistance from a man you did not admire. But you did so to save me."

"I know no man whom I admire more than Sir Ronald." Jack settled his arms around Daphne, drew her to him, and hungrily kissed her.

Afterward, with both of them unaccountably breathless, he spoke in a low, husky voice. "I noticed an inn, Feathers & Leather, just down the street. . ."

The sultry look she gave him sent vibrant life to his groin.

"Where we can . . .?"

He nodded.

$\mathcal{E}$pilogue

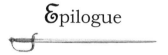

One week later. . .

She heard the front door open and raced down the stairs to greet her husband. "You must tell me everything," Daphne said, throwing her arms around him.

His brows lowered, he eyed her. "Where, madam, are your spectacles?"

Uh oh. She had been married to him long enough to know that when he called her *madam* he was out of charity with her. "I left them off."

"Why?"

"I wanted to be pretty."

"You are prettiest when wearing spectacles." He ran a finger along her nose. "They're part of you, and I like—no, love—everything about you." Pressing a kiss onto her mass of hair, he then took her hand and strolled to the settee in the drawing room.

"Don't feel so badly about the duc getting away," she consoled. "You couldn't have done anything to prevent it."

"More than that, I just don't understand why we cannot find Heff's list."

"I imagine Lord Lambeth threw it away, not knowing its value."

"But Braithwite—the blackguard—confirmed that Lambeth contacted him and told him of its existence."

Mrs. MacInnes entered the chamber to announce the Duchess of Lankersham, but before half the words were out of her mouth, Cornelia swept into the room like a royal personage.

Jack stood and offered her the seat where he had been.

"No. You go ahead and sit by your disgustingly besotted wife." Cornelia moved to an armed chair and elegantly lowered herself into it. Daphne was certain Cornelia had selected that chair because with its high back and arms, it resembled a throne.

This visit was very unusual. Cornelia rarely came to her. She preferred sitting back at her palatial Lankersham House and summoning others to pay her court. "To what do we owe the pleasure?" Daphne asked.

"I was going through the letters. . ."

"The ones to Major Styles?" Daphne asked, her voice low.

There was a forlorn look on Cornelia's face when she answered. "I really was in love with him, you know."

Daphne nodded somberly. "I thought you were."

Cornelia opened her reticule and withdrew a slip of paper. "Before I throw it away, I thought to ask you if this is important. It has the names of six men in government."

Jack leaped up and snatched away the list. His eyes greedily perused the names, and a smile slowly lifted the corners of his mouth. "You, your grace, have performed a great service to your country." He met Daphne's gaze. "I must go to Carlton House at once."

Daphne popped up. "You're not going to see the Regent without me!"

He stopped and smiled down at her. "Our success—Britain's success—would not have been possible without you, Madam Schemer." He eyed the pouting duchess. "The former Chalmers sisters are proving to be invaluable to the crown."

Cornelia, too, rose, her face brightening. "There is one other matter I wished to discuss. To demonstrate the depth of my gratitude to you both, I've bought you a coach. It's outside. I have arranged that the bills for the livery stable be sent to me."

"Oh, your grace," Jack said, "we couldn't possibly--"

"-- not accept something so wonderful!" Daphne finished, moving to hug her sister. "There's nothing I could have either wanted or needed more."

"I have also taken the liberty," Cornelia added, "of engaging the services of that lad the two of you are so excessively fond of. He will remain your coachman."

Jack eyed Daphne, a smile on his face. "By the way, love, Andy said the boots fit perfectly. They're the nicest ones he's ever owned."

Cornelia cleared her throat to command their attention. "Papa, you must know, wouldn't like it above half if you arrived at the Regent's house in a rented hack." She turned up her perfectly shaped nose. "I daresay he'd have apoplexy—and I'm not sure if Lankersham wouldn't, too."

"Papa I can understand," Daphne said, "but I fail to see why it should matter to Lankersham---"

Jack drew his wife into his arms and silenced her with a kiss as Cornelia walked away muttering to herself about the impetuousness of newlyweds.

The End

Author's Biography

A former journalist and English teacher, Cheryl Bolen sold her first book to Harlequin Historical in 1997. That book, *A Duke Deceived*, was a finalist for the Holt Medallion for Best First Book, and it netted her the title Notable New Author. Since then she has published more than 20 books with Kensington/Zebra, Love Inspired Historical and was Montlake launch author for Kindle Serials. As an independent author, she has broken into the top 5 on the *New York Times* and top 20 on the *USA Today* best-seller lists.

Her 2005 book *One Golden Ring* won the Holt Medallion for Best Historical, and her 2011 gothic historical *My Lord Wicked* was awarded Best Historical in the International Digital Awards, the same year one of her Christmas novellas was chosen as Best Historical Novella by Hearts Through History. Her books have been finalists for other awards, including the Daphne du Maurier, and have been translated into eight languages.

She invites readers to www.CherylBolen.com, or her blog, www.cherylsregencyramblings.wordpress.co or Facebook at https://www.facebook.com/pages/Cheryl-Bolen-Books/146842652076424.

Made in the USA
Coppell, TX
08 November 2020

40992396R00150